I0822545

Taos Gothic

Also by James C. Wilson from Sunstone Press:

Hiking New Mexico's Chaco Canyon: The Trails, The Ruins, The History

Santa Fe, City of Refuge: An Improbable Memoir of the Counterculture

New Mexico's Chaco Canyon: Photographing the Ancient City
(A companion to Hiking New Mexico's Chaco Canyon)

The Fernando Lopez Santa Fe Mystery Series:

Peyote Wolf
Smokescreen
Ghost Canyon
The Dead Go Fast
Painted Skull Ranch
Devil On Canyon Road
Taos Vendetta

Taos Gothic

A Fernando Lopez Santa Fe Mystery

James C. Wilson

Santa Fe

Sunstone books may be purchased for educational, business, or sales promotional use.
For information please write: Special Markets Department, Sunstone Press,
P.O. Box 2321, Santa Fe, New Mexico 87504-2321.

eBook 978-1-61139-719-2

Library of Congress Cataloging-in-Publication Data

Names: Wilson, James C., 1948- author. | Wilson, James C., 1948- Fernando Lopez Santa Fe mystery.
Title: Taos gothic : a Fernando Lopez Santa Fe mystery / James C. Wilson.
Description: Santa Fe : Sunstone Press, [2023] | Series: A Fenando Lopez Santa Fe mystery | Summary: "The disappearance of a Santa Fe historian at the historic Mabel Dodge Luhan House in Taos sends private investigator Fernando Lopez on a dangerous journey through a haunted world of ghosts, transients, paranormals, and psychopaths"-- Provided by publisher.
Identifiers: LCCN 2023020283 | ISBN 9781632936172 (hardback) | ISBN 9781611397192 (epub)
Subjects: LCSH: Lopez, Fernando (Fictitious character) | Murder--Investigation--Fiction. | Taos (N.M.)--Fiction.
Classification: LCC PS3623.I58485 T36 2023 | DDC 813.6--dc23/eng/20230509

LC record available at https://lccn.loc.gov/2023020283

WWW.SUNSTONEPRESS.COM
SUNSTONE PRESS / POST OFFICE BOX 2321 / SANTA FE, NM 87504-2321 /USA
(505) 988-4418

Dedicated to the memory of Willa Cather, who with her partner Edith Lewis stayed in the Pink House at the Mabel Dodge Luhan House for two weeks during the summer of 1925 while working on her Santa Fe novel, *Death Comes for the Archbishop.*

The Cather Room

A flash of light woke Kate Isaacs from a deep sleep. The light seemed to come from under the bedroom door. She thrashed about under the blankets before slowly getting her bearings. Now she remembered. She was sleeping in the Cather Room at the Mabel Dodge Luhan House in Taos. For her latest project on Willa Cather. Looking into the 'troubles' that developed between Cather and her lover Edith Lewis when they were staying here in 1925 while Cather researched her masterpiece, *Death Comes for the Archbishop*.

She struggled to free herself from the tangled bedclothes. As she did the light grew brighter, revealing the contours of the small room. The two single beds with a small table and lamp between them. The red Queen Anne chair alongside the yellow flower poster on the wall. The fireplace across the room. Everything glowed in soft focus as if in candlelight. It was called the Cather Room because Cather had slept here on some of her visits.

Suddenly she felt a cold chill sweep into the room. Had she left the door open? She strained her neck to get a view of the door. Closed tight. While she watched the burst of light became a gray vortex spinning upwards into the shape of a human. Frightened, she shrank back against the headboard. The smoky light morphed into the face of a woman. "You—" she said, recognizing the strong, sober face. She opened her mouth to scream but no sound came out.

The apparition floated across the room toward her and extended a long hand, motioning for her to follow. Timid but obeying, she crawled out of bed and slipped into her flip-flops. She wore only a thin nightgown. The door swung open before her and crashed back against the adobe wall. She stepped outside shivering in the cool night air. She took a first, tentative step and then followed the mysterious figure across the porch and toward the gate at the far end of the courtyard. The gigantic cottonwoods and Mabel's birdhouses glistened silver in the moonlight.

"Wait!" she said. "Are you really—?"

She walked trance-like across the rough cobblestones. Was she dreaming? Up ahead the apparition turned to look at her and then disappeared through an open gate in the adobe wall. As she approached a small bell in the gable on top of the wall began to chime, a dull ring that echoed against the adobe. One, two, three chimes. She worried the sound would wake the other guests at the bed-and-breakfast. She had no idea of the time, only that it must be well past Midnight since she remembered leaving Caitlin's party around ten o'clock.

In slow motion she moved through the gate and stopped, looking for her visitor. But the apparition had disappeared, leaving her shivering and standing alone in the moonlight. Above her a thousand stars twinkled in the thin mountain air. She scanned the semi-darkness for any trace, any sign. On her left she saw the faint line of a dirt trail running along the adobe wall toward the rear of the house. She decided to take a chance. She followed the trail carefully, watching her step on the rough terrain so as not to lose her flip-flops.

The trail took her behind the house to a wire fence that separated the Luhan property from land belonging to the one thousand-year-old Taos Pueblo. Had her visitor crossed over or through the fence? She looked for strands of wire that had been pulled apart or places that would provide easy crossing. Maybe the woman lived at the Pueblo. But why would she be haunting the Luhan House at this hour of the night? What did she want?

As her eyes adjusted to the darkness she could see the outlines of the Taos mountains—Wheeler Peak, Simpson Peak, and Blue Mountain with its sacred Blue Lake where the pueblo got its water. Between where she stood and the mountains dozens of lights flashed on and off, sprites dancing in the air. Up close the mesa was pockmarked by the shadows of sage and saltbush, nothing resembling a human form. Maybe she'd imagined her visitor. It was possible, she told herself, because she'd been having nightmares recently about her research and her relationship with Rachel, her wife. And now Caitlin had come back into her life after all these years. What did Caitlin want from her? She rested her hands on the fence while she considered what to do, whether to keep looking or return to her room and go back to sleep.

Then the wind picked up and a dust devil formed on the mesa. The swirling winds blew sand in her face. As she reached for her eyes she heard movement behind her, the sound of someone or something approaching on the trail. As she turned to look she glimpsed a shadowy figure out of the corner of her eye. Suddenly a cloth hood was thrust over her head. She screamed out in fright. Her arms flailed about. She tried to turn around but before she could a drawstring in the hood tightened around her neck, choking off her air.

She panicked, struggling with the cord. The more she struggled the deeper the cord cut into her neck. Her mouth opened in a silent scream as she sank to her knees and then into blackness.

2

Former detective Fernando Lopez decided to take it easy Monday morning. Now that he'd retired from the Santa Fe Police Department to become a private investigator he could take his sweet time. Just last week he'd set up his shingle in the remodeled garage of Ruby Montez's new gallery on Canyon Road. An old friend from the doomed anti-gentrification wars of the nineties, Ruby had let him use the garage rent-free. She'd even allowed him to remodel the small garage into something resembling an office, with wood paneling on the walls and carpet on the concrete floor. With a desk, bookshelves, and two sitting chairs, what else did he need?

He spent the morning drinking coffee and reading the *Independent* on his back patio. Estelle, his wife, asked him run some errands today and start on a list of home repairs she'd prepared for him. She liked to remind him that their small adobe on Acequia Madre was one hundred years old and showing its age. He nodded but didn't intend to do a damned thing around the house anytime soon. His game plan involved spending his mornings at home relaxing and his afternoons at his new office waiting. If no clients showed up, then he would relax at his office too.

After a light lunch he drove his new Jeep Cherokee—a retirement gift from Estelle—down Acequia Madre to the Paseo and around to Canyon Road. His office was located a couple of blocks up from El Farol, the favorite watering hole of the crazy artistic types who lived along Canyon Road. He parked in the gravel lot between Ruby's gallery and Essentia, the sex shop next door. He didn't see Ruby's Honda Accord or any other cars in the parking lot. Ruby split her time between the gallery and her pottery co-op in the Railyard District. Monday, Wednesday, and Friday at the co-op; Tuesday, Thursday, and Saturday at the gallery.

Stepping out of the Cherokee he again had to stop and admire the hand-painted wooden sign at the rear of the parking lot: 'Fernando Lopez, Private Investigator' with an image of an elongated eye below the print. He walked over and opened the door, turning his sign from closed to open. Inside the office still smelled of new wood paneling and carpet. He raised the side window to get some fresh air and then sat down at his desk to admire his latest purchase, a mini refrigerator where he stored bottles of cold water and Modelo, his favorite beer. He thought about adding an easy chair but didn't want the place to look too comfortable, like a man cave or whatever they called it these days.

He was still waiting for his first case as a private investigator, having been open less than a week. That didn't worry him. He knew it would take time to build up the business—if he decided to make it permanent. Meanwhile, he waited. He took out a folder of bills and receipts from his office remodel and began making a spreadsheet of expenses on the laptop he kept in his top drawer. Halfway through the receipts he heard a car door slam outside and then the crunch of footsteps approaching in the gravel parking lot. He looked up to check the identity of his visitor.

A shadow appeared outside the door, a woman. She hesitated a moment and then knocked on the door. "Hello? Is anyone here?"

"Come in. Please."

The door opened, revealing a woman with short red hair split down the center by a blue streak and the palest skin he'd ever seen. She looked like a ghost wearing a red and blue wig, which struck him as odd for a woman of her age, early forties at least. The green sweater and yellow slacks completed the fashion plate that stepped timidly into his office and stared at him.

"Please. Have a seat. How can I help you?"

Without ever taking her eyes off him, she scurried over to the chair facing his desk and sat down, hands in her lap.

"How can I help you?" he asked again.

"Well, my wife is missing. She's disappeared. If you could find her...I mean if that's something you can do, I don't know...."

"Your wife?"

She nodded. "Kate Isaacs. My name is Rachel Wolfe."

"The two of you are married?"

"Yes...does that bother you?" She stared at him.

"Not at all," he reassured her. "Why don't you tell me what happened."

She frowned. "Well, it's a long story. You might know Kate, she's something of a local celebrity. She does the history podcast on famous

New Mexico women. Some of them are well-known, like Georgia O'Keeffe or Mabel Dodge Luhan. Others are lesser known. Like Mary Austin or Carol Stanley or Mary Cabot Wheelwright. Over ten thousand people follow her podcast and the blog she writes to accompany the productions. She also teaches Women's Studies at the UNM branch campus in town. That's where we met. I teach Freshman Composition."

He took a legal pad out of his desk and started taking notes.

She paused long enough for him to finish writing. "Lately she's been working on Willa Cather for her next podcast."

"Willa Cather? She wasn't a New Mexican."

"No, but she spent time in Santa Fe and Taos while she wrote *Death Comes for the Archbishop.* In particular she stayed with Mabel Dodge Luhan in Taos for several weeks while working on the book and then later came back to visit on several occasions. That's why Kate went to Taos. To do research on Cather, who was going to be the subject of her next podcast. The Luhan House is a bed-and-breakfast now, you see. Kate was staying in the Cather Room, a bedroom where Cather sometimes slept on her visits in the nineteen-twenties and thirties. Back when the place was called Los Gallos."

He looked up from his notebook. "So Kate disappeared in Taos? Is that what you're saying?"

"Yes, she didn't answer her phone Sunday morning, so I called the office at the Luhan House and asked them to check on her. They found the door to her room open but no Kate. Apparently she'd gone outside in her nightgown and flip-flops, because her clothes and shoes were found on the other single bed in the room. I drove up Sunday afternoon and found the manager and the Taos County Sheriff going through the room. Looking for clues. But they found nothing, no indication of what happened to her."

'Has she done this before? Disappeared, I mean."

"No, not since we've been married. When we were single she occasionally would go off for a few days with someone else. On a binge. But that changed when we married. We're monogamous now." She glanced at him. "I think."

"You think?"

"Well...as far as I know."

He nodded. "What do you mean she would go off on a 'binge'? Is she a heavy drinker?"

She frowned. "She used to be. And a drug user. On occasion."

"What kind of drugs?"

She threw up her hands. "You name it. Meth, Oxy, weed. Maybe even the hard stuff. I don't know because I wasn't involved and Kate never wanted to discuss her 'flings,' as she called them."

"Did you or the others find any drugs in her room at the Luhan House?"

She shook her head. "No."

"So what did the Taos Sheriff say when you talked to him?"

She shrugged. "Not much. He had me file a missing person report and told me not to worry, that tourists who wander off usually come back soon enough. He wasn't very helpful. One of those macho cowboy types."

"I know Hank Mathews. He's rough around the edges but a good cop. Has anything turned up since yesterday?"

She lowered her head. Tears welled in her eyes and then began to streak down her face.

"I guess not."

She opened her purse looking for a tissue.

"Sorry, but I have to ask you a few more questions," he said, and waited for her to compose herself.

She nodded.

"Does she have any enemies...anyone she might have quarreled with...who might want to harm her?"

She shook her head, drying her eyes. "Not that I'm aware of. I mean, she's a teacher. She doesn't make many enemies. Same with her history podcasts. I can't imagine."

He considered. "Did she mention any side trips or places around Taos she might be visiting while she was there?"

She shook her head. "Not really. She was only there for a few hours before she disappeared. How would she have had time for a side trip?"

"Fair enough," he said. "What about friends in Taos? Could someone have picked her up Saturday night?"

Rachel's face turned red. She shook her head.

Fernando noticed her agitation and dropped the subject. "Okay. I can drive up to Taos this afternoon and see what I can find out." He opened a drawer and took out a copy of his rate sheet. "Here are my rates. I'll need a retainer today and then I'll bill you for the rest."

"Thank you."

He handed her a legal pad. "Write down your phone numbers. I'll call you tonight."

She wrote down her cell and home phone numbers and passed the pad back to him. Then she took a checkbook out of her purse and wrote the check. She hesitated a moment and then handed him the check.

"Do you think you can find her today?"

He stifled a laugh. Everyone wanted instant results. "I'll see what I can do. Like I said, I'll call you tonight."

She rose tentatively out of the chair, looked at him for a brief moment and then nodded. Without another word she walked out of the office.

He went to the window and watched her get into her car, a fairly new BMW parked behind his Cherokee. A good sign. If she could afford to drive a Beamer, she could afford to pay his fee.

First things first. He found his cell phone, opened his Contacts list and clicked on Hank Mathews.

"Howdy Fernando!" boomed the big voice. "Long time no see. What's shakin' down there in Santa Fe?"

"Hey, Hank. I'm calling about this Kate Isaacs woman who disappeared from the Mabel Dodge Luhan House Saturday night. What have you found out so far?"

"Hah! Not a damned thing. She just walked out of her bedroom in the middle of the night and disappeared. Her car is still in the parking lot. We don't know if someone came by and picked her up or what the hell happened to her. Doesn't look like a kidnapping."

"No evidence of foul play?"

"None. We searched the grounds and then drove up and down Morada Lane and the other nearby streets but found nothing. Nada. Why do you ask?"

"The woman's partner just left my office. She wants me to find Kate."

"Did she file a missing person report down there too?" Hank asked.

"No, I'm not at the station," Fernando said. "I guess I haven't told you. I took early retirement and set up as a private investigator. She's my first customer. Wants me to find Kate today."

"Yeah! Wouldn't it be nice!"

"Rachel's her name, the partner."

"Oh yeah, she came up Sunday afternoon. A quiet one, didn't say much. Seemed to think I was keeping something from her or not doing my job, whatever. We didn't hit it off."

"Anyway, I'm on my way up. Should be there in a couple of hours."

"Well, don't stay at the Luhan House whatever you do."

"What do you mean?"

"Weird things been happening out there, that's what I mean. Been in the news lately. Lots of complaints. People hearing screams and gunshots and the like. Bunch of so-called paranormals have posted recordings of voices taken during night in the Luhan House. Got people all riled up."

"Voices?"

"Ghosts! These guys claim to have recorded the voices of Mabel and her husband Tony and God knows who else. Even the voices of Dennis Hopper and some of the other hippies who lived there in the crazy seventies."

Fernando let that sink in for a few seconds. "So...have these ghosts, whatever they are, caused any harm? Have there been other disappearances or incidents of foul play?"

"No, just people reporting unusual sights and sounds...being scared, basically. My guess is they're hearing the old house creak. That old abode house is more than a hundred years old, spliced together in different wings and levels. No wonder it makes sounds."

"What about the sightings?"

"You tell me, I don't know what the hell to make of them. People's imaginations, I guess."

"Okay...I might see you this afternoon," Fernando said. "If not, let's keep in touch."

"Will do. I'll give you a call if anything turns up."

3

Fernando took the low road to Taos. Highway 68 ran alongside the Rio Grande as it meandered though one canyon after another. The river remained high from the Spring runoff. Approaching Velarde he saw trailers stacked with boats in the roadside parking areas, with kayakers and white water rafters already in the river. He slowed down to take a closer look but decided against stopping, given the lateness of the hour. He kept thinking about Rachel's story. It made no sense that Kate would get out of bed in the middle of the night and step outside in her nightgown and walk away. People didn't just disappear into thin air. Someone must have picked her up, a friend or former lover, someone. He didn't know what to think about Hank's comments about ghosts and paranormals.

Minutes later he crested the last hill and drove by the Ranchos de Taos church, famously painted and photographed by more artists than he could count. The highway stretched out as far as the eye could see, with Taos sprawled on either side of the highway and the 13,000-foot peaks of the Taos Ski Basin straight ahead. He ignored the fast food restaurants and the other commercial claptrap and drove into the heart of the old city, turning right at the Plaza intersection onto Kit Carson Road and then left onto Morada Lane.

The Mable Lodge Luhan House appeared on his right. The name was a bit deceptive because the property included multiple buildings. The big adobe house, built on a slight rise, overlooked several smaller buildings below, some used for guests and others idle and in a state of disrepair. He turned into the large parking area, empty except for a couple of cars parked near the stairs up to the big house and a blue Passat seemingly stranded all by itself in the middle of the parking lot. He'd been here a few times over the years beginning in the 1970s when Dennis

Hopper owned the property. He and a couple of his pot-head friends from Santa Fe High would come up on weekends to party with the artists and hippies that hung out with Hopper. Back when he was single, a million years ago.

He parked and walked up the stairs into the courtyard of the big house, a sprawling century-old adobe structure that contained some two dozen rooms on the first and second levels. A partial third level, Mabel's bedroom, rose above the rest of the house like a tower, complete with rows of blank windows overlooking the grounds. Vegas, chimneys, and iron weather vanes cluttered the roof creating a bizarre, slightly ominous look. He had the same reaction every time he saw the house. It looked as if the house had no design but was instead assembled one level and one wing at a time by someone who happened to be mad.

The sidewalk took him up to a long porch under a veranda. He stepped inside a corner doorway and entered the central part of the house—sitting room, dining room, and kitchen, all appointed with furnishings that looked decades old. To the right of the sitting room he spotted a woman sitting at a desk in what passed for an office, a tiny room no bigger than a walk-in closet with a desk, book shelves, and file cabinets crammed into the small space.

"Hello, can I help you?" she asked, an older woman with short gray hair wearing a tailored black suit. Her nametag identified her as Francis Rose.

"Fernando Lopez," he introduced himself, handing her a card. "I've been hired to investigate the disappearance of Kate Isaacs this past Saturday.

"Oh yes, Rachel called earlier and said you'd be coming," she said, walking over to greet him. "I'm Francis. Let me show you the Cather Room. The police left everything as they found it, not knowing when or if Kate would be coming back. Her car hasn't moved from the parking lot. It's the blue Volkswagen Passat if you want to take a look."

"Thanks, I saw the car on my way in," he said. "Did you have any interactions with Kate? Did she seem stressed, or worried, or anything that raised a red flag with you?"

"No, she seemed fine. I checked her in Saturday afternoon when she arrived, but I don't think I saw her after that. Oh wait, she did stop by once asking if she could have a tour of the Pink House. I told her it was closed to the public."

"What's the Pink House?"

"That's where Willa Cather stayed on one of her longer visits. I think she wrote part of *Death Comes for the Archbishop* there."

He followed her outside to the long porch and down to the Cather Room, which had a police notice on the door. She took a key out of her pocket and unlocked the door, allowing him to enter first. A large window with white lace curtains provided enough light for him to see the room clearly. The single bed where Kate had slept was unmade, its bedclothes tangled on the floor, while the other single hadn't been touched. He looked around the room, finding Kate's clothes and shoes in the closet. On a small table beside the stuffed chair he found her cellphone, uncharged. On the bureau he found a hardback copy of *Utopian Vistas*, a book about the Mabel Dodge Luhan House and a leather portfolio.

He turned to Francis and asked, "Could you excuse me?"

She blushed. "Of course. Just close the door when you're finished. It'll lock automatically."

After she left he sat down in the chair and opened the portfolio. He found page after page of notes, mostly names, dates, and information about Willa Cather's time in New Mexico. Some comments about her novels, especially *Death Comes for the Archbishop,* but also what Kate referred to as the 'dark' novels, *The Professor's House* and *A Lost Lady*. Toward the end he found several pages of Kate's random impressions of staying in the Cather Room and eating in the same dining room where Cather and her partner Edith Lewis had dined. Impressionistic, stream of consciousness writing that proved difficult to read. On the last page Kate recorded her frustration over being denied access to the Pink House, where the "intrigue" was supposed to have occurred. Just what kind of "intrigue" wasn't explained. The last line in the portfolio, scribbled in large hurried letters, was the name Caitlin and a phone number.

Maybe this Caitlin person came by Saturday night. He wondered if this might be the break they needed.

Using his cellphone camera, he photographed the pages that seemed relevant and put the portfolio back where he found it. Then he looked to make sure Francis had gone back to the office. Satisfied, he tore through the room, opening drawers and raising mattresses and looking in and under every piece of furniture. Searching for drugs or evidence of drug use. He found nothing, not even a stray joint. As far as he could tell the room was clean.

He sat down on the stuffed chair and dialed Caitlin's number. After two rings a message cut off the ringing: "You've reached Caitlin...I'm not here, so leave a message and I'll call you back ASAP. Promise."

With that he left the room, locking the door behind him. He walked across the patio and down to the parking lot, looking for what he didn't know. He stopped first at Kate's car, the blue Passat. The doors and trunk were locked, so he took out his pick and helped himself. Inside he found a couple of joints in the glove compartment and an empty coffee travel mug in the center cup holder. On the rear seat he saw several Cather novels tossed on top of a light jacket. So he climbed out of the Passat and opened the trunk, finding a Nikon camera bag, heavy with camera, and a small thermal cooler filled with soft drinks. Nothing helpful.

He closed the trunk and made sure the car doors were locked. Then he came back to the patio and walked slowly to the side entrance, an adobe arch with a bell gable on top. He noticed a dirt trail running alongside the wall to the left, toward the rear of the Luhan House. And something else. Slide marks in the dirt, which could have been made by someone wearing flip-flops. Someone like Kate.

He followed the dirt trail, looking for anything that would provide a clue. While walking he heard the roar of a chainsaw chewing up brush behind the house. The slide marks ended at a barbed wire fence that marked the beginning of Taos Pueblo land. The footprints just stopped. He saw none of the marks beyond the fence or on either side of the trail. What he did see was a patch of churned up dirt as if a struggle had occurred there. That might explain why there were no slide marks going back toward the side entrance. None.

"*Hola!*" someone shouted.

He turned and saw two men cutting brush farther down the fence line. One, a tall Anglo, held a smoking chainsaw in his hands. The other, an Indian, stood with both hands on top of a rake watching him. The Anglo waved.

He walked through the overgrown sage bushes along the fence to where the two men worked.

"You looking for something?" the Anglo asked.

"I'm a private investigator. I'm looking for the woman in the Cather Room who disappeared Saturday night. Kate Isaacs."

"Hah! Good luck with that. Who knows where she went."

Fernando gave the man a curious look. "Why do you say that?"

"Because this place is haunted. People disappear here all the time. Poof, they're gone. Just like that."

"Fernando Lopez," he introduced himself, holding out his hand and ignoring the haunted reference.

"Tom Jensen," the man responded and shook hands. Tall and gangly with a long ponytail just starting to gray, he looked like an old Taos hippie from the 1970s. He wore a Dodgers baseball cap and a matching blue kerchief around his neck.

"Did you happen to see Kate Saturday?"

"Yeah, I saw her when she checked in. I offered to carry her bag but she said she didn't need any help. Looked offended. Not very friendly."

"What about later on? Did you see her Saturday night?"

Tom nodded. "She was standing outside her room when I got off work. I didn't know if she was going for a walk or waiting for someone to pick her up. I asked if she needed a ride. She said she was on her way to a party on Kit Carson, so I said hop in. I dropped her off at the address she gave me and that was it. I never saw her again."

"Do you remember the address?" Fernando asked.

Tom took his cell phone out of his back pocket and checked. "Here...I wrote it down in case I had to pick her up later."

Fernando made a note of the address on Kit Carson. "So did you pick her up later, after the party?"

"No, she never called, so I forgot about her."

"Do you know who lives this address? Who Kate was visiting?"

"No, I didn't go inside," Tom said, laughing, "I wasn't invited."

"What about you?" Fernando addressed the Indian, who was looking off into the distance as if he hadn't heard a word of the conversation. The Indian was considerably older than Tom, with a dark wrinkled face and sunglasses concealing his eyes.

"Jim don't talk to strangers," Tom explained. "Never says a word. Long as I've known him."

Fernando took a card out of his back pocket and handed it to Tom. "Well if you come across anything, give me a call. Be much appreciated."

"Will do, but I can tell you what probably happened to her. The ghosts took her. They're raising all sorts of hell around here. I could tell you stories that would make your hair stand on end. I'm serious. Ask anyone who works here. They'll tell you the same thing."

"No kidding? So then you've seen the ghosts?" Fernando asked.

"Only after dark. That's why I try to get out of here before sunset. Stop by sometime and I'll tell you some stories. I can't talk now. I have to finish here."

"I might do that," he said, turning to walk away.

"Consider yourself warned," Tom called after him.

4

By the time Fernando finished inspecting the grounds of the Luhan House the sun was sinking fast in the western sky leaving a smudge of crimson on the horizon. He figured he had less than an hour of daylight remaining. That meant it was crunch time—time to make a decision. He could race back to Santa Fe and return tomorrow morning, or he could stay the night in Taos and maybe, with a bit of luck, finish his business tomorrow.

He decided to stay. How difficult could it be to find an Anglo woman tourist wearing a nightgown and flip-flops? She would stand out like a sore thumb no matter where she turned up.

He returned to his Cherokee and drove back to the Plaza intersection, turning right onto Paseo del Pueblo Norte. Five blocks up he pulled into the El Pueblo Lodge, where he'd stayed just last year while chasing Jimmy Mackey all over northern New Mexico. A 1960s motor lodge with small rooms and aging furniture, the place left a lot to be desired. But it was inexpensive and centrally located. Tonight the El Pueblo looked deserted with only two cars parked in the lot, an indication that tourist season hadn't started yet. By May the place would be jumping.

He walked into the office and found a young woman with short-cropped hair and a nose ring behind the front counter. Bored, she looked up from the book she was reading and frowned. "Yes?"

"I'd like a room—the one on the end. I stayed there last fall."

"For one night?"

He laughed. "I sure hope so."

She frowned again but made the reservation and handed him the keycard. "Breakfast at seven."

He moved the Cherokee in front of his unit and walked into the familiar room. Two queens, a wobbly table, and a couple of uncomfortable chairs. He threw his duffel bag on one of the beds and sat down to text Estelle. He didn't want to call her because he knew she would give him a hard time for spending the night in Taos. A text would avoid another argument. Then he tried Caitlin's number with the same result as before. No answer. So he called Rachel back in Santa Fe hoping she could tell him something about Caitlin.

"Yes?" came the tentative voice.

"Fernando," he announced. "I'm still in Taos. I went through Kate's room at the Luhan House this afternoon. I didn't find any drugs or evidence of foul play, nothing that would explain her disappearance. Tell me, did she ever mention ghosts at the Luhan House?"

"Sure, she was aware of the ghost stories and the research. She wanted to find out if the voices the paranormals had recorded in the house included Cather's. If so, that would make a great lead-in to the Cather podcast. New communications from Willa Cather!"

Fernando considered. "Is that what she was investigating? The ghosts?"

Rachel paused. "Well...that and the love triangles."

"Love triangles? What do you mean?"

Rachel paused again. "You do know that Cather and Edith Lewis were lovers, right? Well, it seems both of them were also attracted to Mabel...and to Tony. No one at the Luhan House back then was monogamous. They believed in free love...and that freedom tempted Cather and Lewis, who were otherwise a pretty staid, conservative couple. Kate found some passages in Cather's letters and her published writing about Tony that piqued her interest."

"I found a note in Kate's portfolio that mentioned the 'intrigue' that started when Cather and Lewis stayed in the Pink House," Fernando said. "So that's what she was referring to? The love triangles?"

"Yes, and the psychic damage they caused Cather," Rachel said. "Kate believed the damage is reflected in the conflict between Archbishop Lamy and Father Antonio José Martinez of Taos in *Death Comes for the Archbishop* and why Cather didn't publish another novel for another four years, an exceptionally long time for her. If you remember the book, Martinez had fathered several children and didn't believe in the celibacy of the clergy."

"How does this explain Cather's so-called 'psychic damage'?"

"Because Cather was conflicted. She was both attracted to and fearful of sexual profligacy. Same with Kate. That's one of the reasons she was interested in Cather. Monogamy didn't come easy for Kate. I think that's why Kate spent so much time on her research–it was a way to sublimate her sexual desires. To be honest, I just couldn't satisfy her libido."

When Fernando didn't respond, she continued. "What about you, Detective Lopez? Have you always been monogamous?"

"Well...for the most part," he said, wondering how they'd ended up talking about their sex lives.

"There you go," Rachel responded.

He didn't know what to say about that so he said nothing. "Okay. I also need to ask you about something else. Who's Caitlin?"

"Why do you want to know?"

"Because I found a message in Kate's portfolio to call Caitlin."

Silence at the other end.

"Hello? Are you still there?" Fernando asked.

"Yes...Caitlin's an old friend of Kate's...actually, an old lover... before we were together."

"Tell me what you know about her."

"She's bad news, a doper. She's the one who got Kate hooked on drugs back when they were together. Kate swore she would never have anything to do with Caitlin again. Are you saying they got together?"

"I don't know," he said. "I'm still trying to get in touch with Caitlin. She doesn't answer her phone."

"Oh great!"

"What does Caitlin do—other than drugs."

"Hah! What doesn't she do? She refers to herself as a midwife, a masseuse, and an herb doctor. She grows her own herbs and supposedly uses ancient Hispanic and Native American remedies to treat all sorts of illnesses. In other words she's a con-woman, a shyster. Typical of Taos hippies!"

"Do you know where she lives?"

"Yeah...I can't remember the name of the street. It's a little street off Kit Carson Road. You'll have to look it up."

"Okay. I'll let you know if I find Kate."

Before he did anything else he decided to walk down the block to Michael's Kitchen, the funky restaurant that had been a Taos staple for fifty years. Everything else could wait. He was hungry.

As usual Michael's was packed with locals in their flannel shirts, scruffy jeans and hiking boots. The Taos look. He found a table in back and waited for the server, a plump woman with a warm smile. She started to hand him a menu but he waved it away and said, "I'll have the Chicken Enchilada Plate with red chile and a Modelo."

"You got it, honey," she said, scribbling down the order and heading for the kitchen.

He ate quickly, left a twenty dollar bill on the table, and stepped outside just as his cell phone rang. He recognized the voice immediately.

"Howdy, Fernando...it's Hank. Are you still in Taos?"

"Yeah, just leaving Michael's Kitchen."

"Well, you might want to come over and take a look at this. I've got a situation here, a homicide. Looks like your Kate Isaacs is involved."

"Okay, where are you?"

"We're at five forty Ortega Road. Just go east on Kit Carson for a mile or thereabouts and turn left on Ortega. Look for the squad car and all the lights. You can't miss it."

"I'm on my way."

He stopped at his room long enough to use the bathroom and then headed out Kit Carson. The fading light of a blood red sunset made it difficult to see the narrow, winding road. He drove past Ortega the first time and had to backtrack. Like Hank said, the house proved easy to find once he was on the correct street. Yard lights illuminated a large patio in front of the house. He saw Hank's cruiser and a forensics van parked in the driveway. Across the street a bunch of neighbors gawked at the police scene from the shadows.

Fernando set the brake and left his cruiser on the street and walked up the driveway. The small frame house had a clerestory on one side and a bank of tall windows in front, with solar panels on top of the roof. He noticed Hank standing on the patio talking to a small woman wrapped in a shawl. He waved from a distance and then joined them on the patio. The woman looked nervous standing next to Hank, which wasn't surprising. Hank often had that effect on people, what with his wide-brimmed Stetson and his Texas drawl.

"This here is Claudia Roybal, the neighbor who reported the crime," Hank said.

Claudia nodded. "Like I told him, I first noticed the smell Sunday. Today it was worse so I thought maybe a large animal had died. But when I came over this afternoon I realized the smell was coming from inside the house. That's when I called nine one one."

Hank nodded. "Can you stay a bit? I need to show Fernando around."

"Sure." She took at seat on one of the patio chairs and folded her arms across her chest.

The sharp odor of a decaying body stung his nostrils as Fernando stepped inside the house. He followed Hank, noticing the tie-dye curtains on the windows and the brightly painted folk art on the walls. Potted plants and herbs lined the windowsills, while cheap Mexican rugs covered the floors and the two sofas in the sitting room. The glasses and empty bottles of wine on the kitchen counter suggested a recent party. So, too, did the ashtray, stuffed with clay pipes and roaches.

Hank motioned him over to a coffee table. "Take a look at this."

He examined the ragged lines of white powder on the tabletop.

Then he saw the card. A plastic credit card apparently used to cut the white powder. He read the name on the card: Kate Isaacs.

"So Kate was here."

"Yessir, Saturday night. Claudia said she heard them partying."

Hank pulled a kerchief out of his back pocket and held it over his nose. "Let me show you the rest."

He followed Hank into a study, with a desk and computer and bookshelves along the walls. He found a masked tech from the forensics van shooting photos of the corpse. She lay sprawled on the floor near a filing cabinet, a woman with long black hair curled around her head and an India print skirt bunched at her waist. Her legs were twisted under her as though she had fallen in that position. He saw the wound, congealed with black blood, on the left side of her head. The sight of her made him gag as much as the smell.

"Who is she?" Fernando asked.

"Adams...Caitlin Adams."

"Caitlin? No kidding."

"Why's that? You looking for her too?"

"I found a note in Kate's room at the Luhan House to call Caitlin. I 'm assuming this is the Caitlin."

Fernando quickly left the room and went outside. He wanted more information about the party Saturday night. Claudia looked away when she saw him coming, still uncomfortable.

"I told Chief Mathews all I know," she said, as if to ward him off. Her face was partly hidden by shadows.

"Can you tell me? Please."

"All I know is that Caitlin had a party over here Saturday night. Not that many people, only five or so. They were loud, playing music and talking, but no more than usual. It didn't seem like anything out of the ordinary. I heard some screaming later on, maybe eleven o'clock or Midnight. Woke me up. But it didn't last long, so I went back to sleep. That's all I remember."

"Do you know who the other people were?" Fernando asked. "Did you see any of them?"

"Not really. I heard Caitlin's boyfriend, Billy Jackson. And I saw a couple of women get out of a car early on when I was working in the garden. Another car drove up later, after I went inside. I didn't get a good look at any of them."

"What about the screaming you heard? Sometime between eleven o'clock and Midnight, you say?"

She nodded.

"How long did it go on?"

"Not long. I didn't think much about it because Caitlin and Billy fought all the time. I don't know why they were together. They didn't seem to agree on much of anything. All they did was fight."

"Who is this guy, Billy?" Fernando asked.

"He works as a guide for one of the companies that give raft and kayak rides on the Rio Grande down at Pilar. Seasonal work."

"Which company?"

"Something to do with 'adventures.' I can't remember the name."

As they talked Fernando heard a man shouting next door. It slowly dawned on him that the man was shouting at them. He turned to see a short but powerfully built man walking across the grass toward them. He guessed correctly that it was Claudia's husband.

"Get over here! Now!" he yelled at his wife.

"I'm coming!" she yelled back.

The burly man approached with balled fists. "Leave her alone! She's told you everything she knows! I want her to stay away from these perverts! Lesbians, trans, whatever the hell they call themselves, we want nothing to do with them! Do you understand?"

"No problem," Fernando said to defuse the situation. "She was just telling us what she saw. A woman was murdered inside."

"No great loss!" he snapped.

Claudia gave Fernando an apologetic look and then followed her husband across the empty lot to their house.

Moments later Hank came outside. "What y'all yelling about out here?"

"Claudia's husband," Fernando said. "He wasn't happy we were keeping his wife."

"Yeah, that's Mark. He's always had a burr in his saddle. Can't blame him, I suppose. He works for the National Forest Service, sometimes as a fire fighter. Overworked and underpaid. Damn hard work."

"I'll keep that in mind," Fernando said.

Hank listened to the Roybals arguing next door and frowned. "No need for you to stick around. I'll stay until forensics finishes and call you tomorrow if I have any other news. Now we'll for damn sure have to find this Kate Isaacs."

Fernando nodded. "Yes we will."

With that, he walked down the driveway to his Cherokee and drove back to the El Pueblo. He didn't bother to turn on the lights in his room. Dog tired, he kicked off his shoes and collapsed on the nearest bed.

5

Fernando woke up with an aching back and a bad attitude as soon as he remembered where he was: on a sagging mattress at El Pueblo Lodge. The same exact feeling he had the last time he woke up here. For a few moments he was sorry he'd come out of retirement to become a private investigator. He missed his quiet home on Acequia Madre. The world could go to hell as far as he was concerned. All he really wanted from life, what time he had left, was his quiet corner of Santa Fe.

Grumbling to himself, he fumbled with the automatic coffee maker in the bathroom. The coffee, though weak, improved his mood. At least he could think clearly. He would give this one more day and see if he could find Kate Isaacs. Hah! He wasn't asking for much, was he? Especially now that Caitlin's murder complicated the case. The only lead he had at the moment was Billy Jackson, the on-again, off-again boyfriend of Caitlin who reportedly worked for a rafting company with the word 'adventure' in its name. Finding Billy would be his first order of business.

He washed his face and brewed himself another cup of lukewarm coffee. Then he sat down with his coffee and cell phone and googled rafting companies in Taos. He scanned the list until he came to one that caught his eye: Taos Great River Rafting Adventures, located on the highway into town. That had to be the one. He hoped.

He dialed the number and got an immediate response: "Great River Rafting Adventures, Jen speaking."

"Yeah, I'm calling Billy Jackson. Is he available?"

"Billy? May I ask whose calling?"

"Fernando Lopez. I'm a friend of a friend," he lied. "I wanted to ask him a few questions about rafting up north in Rio Grande del Norte."

"Oh...well, he's already out for the day...loading up at the yard. He'll be at the loading ramp in Pilar by ten. That's when his first tour is scheduled to depart."

"Okay, thanks," he said and clicked off.

That would give him time to eat breakfast at Michael's Kitchen and check with Hank on any recent developments.

He walked down to Michael's, taking his time eating an order of Huevos Rancheros with extra green chile. Then he came back to his room and called Hank, who didn't answer. So he left a message asking Hank to call him back if there was anything new to report this morning. Afterwards he killed time reading the *Albuquerque Journal* and then at 9:30 headed out to Pilar.

Once past Ranchos de Taos the highway curved around to the west and then back to the east as it entered Piedra Lumbre and Agua Caliente canyons. He drove by the Rio Grande Gorge Visitor Center and followed the river down to Pilar. He noticed several cars parked in the gravel pull-off, but the Great River Rafting Adventures trailer carrying the rafts and kayaks hadn't yet arrived. So he parked off to the side of the lot and waited. A few minutes later he heard the trailer clanking over the rough highway.

He stood back and watched as a heavy duty Ford-350 pickup turned into the lot. Behind it came the trailer loaded with a colorful assortment of rafts and kayaks. He waited until the truck and trailer swung around and backed up near the river before walking over to the rig. The driver, who turned out to be Billy Jackson, climbed out of the cab and noticed him approaching.

Billy was a tall wiry fellow with a muscular build and a permanently sunburned face. He wore a baseball cap, jeans and a 'Great River Rafting Adventures' sweatshirt.

"Billy Jackson?" he asked.

"That's me. What can I do for you?"

"I'm a friend of Kate Isaacs," Fernando said. "I'd like to ask you a few questions about the party at Caitlin Adams' house Saturday. Turns out Caitlin was murdered that night."

"Yeah...I heard on the radio this morning."

"Is there somewhere we could talk?"

Billy looked around. "Sure, I have a few minutes before my first customers arrive. Let's go over to the picnic table.

He followed Billy to a picnic table in a stand of trees beside the lot. Billy looked at him warily from across the table. "Are you a cop?"

"No, I'm a private investigator. Looking for Kate. She seems to have disappeared."

"How so?"

Fernando told Billy about Kate's disappearance from the Cather Room at the Luhan House. "Did you see her at the party Saturday? We know she was there."

"Yeah, I saw her. She was already there when I arrived. I didn't see her car, so someone must have given her a ride. Or I suppose she could have walked. It's not that far from the Luhan House."

"Who else attended the party?"

"Just the three of us and the Baca twins. It wasn't really a party, just old friends getting together."

"The Baca twins?"

Billy nodded. "They're identical twins, Kirsten and Susan. They both work at the Planned Parenthood on Bent Street."

"What time did you leave Caitlin's house?" Fernando asked.

"Right after the twins left. Must have been about ten. Why are you asking? What's this all about? I don't know anything about what happened to Kate. She was with Caitlin when I left."

"Do you have someone who can vouch for you? After you left the party?"

"Wait...I don't like the sound of this," Billy said, getting up from the picnic table.

"You were Caitlin's boyfriend," Fernando responded. "The two of you fought nonstop. We have witnesses who will testify to that. You're going to be the chief suspect, so why don't you tell me what you know about the murder. Maybe I can help you."

"Jesus Christ! I didn't kill her. I left with the Baca twins, you can ask them. And I wasn't really Caitlin's boyfriend. I mean, we slept together from time to time, but shit, that doesn't make me her boyfriend. We were too different. Like you say, we fought all the time. She was bi-sexual, but her preference was really lesbian, for fuck's sake. You know that, right? She and Kate Isaacs were lovers back in the day. Maybe they still are. Hell, they were kissing and making out at the party Saturday night. They're both lesbians!"

Fernando stared at him. "They were getting intimate?"

"Yes. Now leave me alone. I don't have anything more to say."

Billy turned away and walked back to his truck. He started unbuckling the straps holding the rafts and kayaks on the trailer.

Fernando stayed at the picnic table watching as more Great River Rafting Adventures workers drove up and began unloading equipment.

The workers had the first rafts in the water and equipped with provisions and life jackets by the time the rafters on the early tours arrived. Soon the parking lot filled with cars and people, too many people for Fernando's comfort. As he walked to his Cherokee he noticed Billy watching him from behind the trailer. Every step of the way.

Fernando drove back into Taos, parking at the Plaza and walking down to the Starbuck's for his morning exercise. He ordered a tall coffee and took it outside to a table. He planned to pay a visit to the Baca twins next. After that, he didn't know.

His cell phone rang while he sipped his coffee. He recognized Hank's voice immediately.

"Fernando, old buddy, I do have some news for you this morning. Seems Caitlin fell and hit her head on a metal filing cabinet Saturday night. Maybe while struggling with someone. We got the names of the people at the party from Claudia next door. No thanks to her husband, who wouldn't say a damned thing. Yeah, he's one disagreeable sonofabitch. I'm guessing you already have those names and are making the rounds. We won't get around to it until this afternoon. One of those days."

"I am," Fernando said. "Claudia gave me the same information. The names of the other three people at the party—Billy Jackson and the Baca twins. I just talked to Jackson down at Pilar. He seemed nervous. Didn't do or say anything that would persuade me to eliminate him as a suspect."

"I hear you. We've had our run-ins with Billy Jackson. Here's the thing, though. Claudia mentioned five people. Those three plus Caitlin and your Kate Isaacs. But forensics found six sets of fingerprints and DNA on the wine glasses and the joints left in the ashtrays. You hear me? Six people were at that party, not five. So who's our missing man...or woman?"

That gave Fernando pause. Maybe someone came later, after the others had gone. Claudia said she heard a car pull up to Caitlin's house late. Maybe Billy Jackson is protecting someone. Claudia, too, for that matter. He intended to find out.

He chose not to share his thoughts with Hank. Better to wait until he knew more.

"Good question," Fernando said.

6

A nondescript red brick building, the Planned Parenthood Center looked like a small dental or doctor's office from a time when such private offices existed. The place stood back from the street as if wanting to be left alone. Fernando saw only one protestor on the sidewalk: an old man sleeping in a folding chair. Without any prospective patients to harass at the moment the old geezer had fallen asleep, snoring and snorting loudly. His long, unkempt white hair made him look like Santa Claus without the red suit. Propped up against his chair was a sign that read 'Abortion is Murder.'

Fernando walked quietly past the old man, not wanting to wake him. He certainly didn't want to listen to the old man's rant.

A bell rang when he opened the front door and stepped inside. He found an empty waiting room with no one at the front counter. "I'm sorry, we're on lunch break," said a disembodied voice from somewhere. He turned to find a small dark-haired woman with glasses looking at him from the door to a side room. She seemed more curious than irritated at his intrusion.

"Hello. I'm here to see Kirsten and Susan Baca."

"I'm Susan," she said, wiping a strand of hair out of her eyes. "What can I do for you?"

"Good. I'm looking for Kate Isaacs. She's been missing since Saturday. I understand you and your sister attended a party with her that night. I wonder if I could ask you a couple of questions."

Suddenly another small, dark-haired woman with glasses appeared in the doorway. He thought he was seeing double.

"I'm Kirsten," the second woman said. "I'll let Susan answer your questions. I would tell you exactly the same thing. We're identical twins."

Fernando laughed. "So I see."

Kirsten disappeared, leaving him alone with Susan.

"Was Kate already at the party when you arrived?" Fernando asked.

"Yeah, she was inside with Caitlin when we arrived."

"Do you remember seeing Kate's car, a blue VW Passat?"

Susan thought for a moment. "You know, I don't. I remember seeing Caitlin's car. And Billy Jackson's car. He came right after we did."

"Why did the party break up?" he asked. "Was it because Billy and Caitlin were arguing?"

"Not exactly, but they were starting to argue. Billy caught Caitlin and Kate kissing out on the patio. The neighbor saw them too, that Roybal guy next door. He was screaming at them, calling them lesbians and perverts. Billy heard the screaming and came out to see what was going on. Then he started in on Caitlin too. He could get possessive because Caitlin was a free spirit. It wasn't much fun to be around them when they got like that."

"Did they get violent? Hurt each other?" Fernando asked.

She shook her head. "Not when we were there. Just a lot of yelling."

"So when the yelling started you and your sister left, but Kate stayed...is that right?"

"Yeah. The fighting didn't seem to bother Kate. Maybe she was used to it, I don't know."

"One more question," Fernando said. "In addition to you and Kirsten and the people we've mentioned, was anyone else at the party?"

"No. Not that I saw. Unless that Roybal guy came over after we left. He was pretty worked up."

"The reason I ask is that police found six sets of fingerprints on the glasses," Fernando said. "We've only identified five of the people so far."

Susan shook her head. "I really have no idea."

He took a card out of his back pocket and handed it to her. "Please call me if you think of anything else."

He walked outside into the fresh spring air. The old man still snored peacefully in his folding chair. Otherwise he didn't see anyone on the street.

Fernando took his time driving back to the Luhan House. What now? He parked in the lot and walked up the steps to the courtyard. He saw Francis talking to one of the maids in the front office. Looked like she was scolding the maid, a young Native American woman who looked bedraggled and brow-beaten by the older woman. He waited until they were finished before walking across the patio and into the front sitting room.

Francis smiled when she saw him. "You're still here, I see. Would you like a room?"

He laughed. "I may need one if I stay any longer."

"So you haven't found her?"

"Nope. Do you know if any of the staff talked to her after she checked in with you?"

"Not that I'm aware of," she said. "I mean, she checked in about four p.m. and disappeared that night. I'm not sure if anyone else even saw her."

Fernando frowned. "Tom did. I talked to him yesterday. He said he saw Kate standing outside her room when he left for the night. And that he gave her a ride to a party at Caitlin Adams' house."

"Caitlin, the woman who was murdered?" Francis asked. "I heard something about that on the news this morning."

"Exactly. You see the problem."

"What else did Tom say?" Francis asked.

"Not much. He wished me luck finding her. Warned me about the ghosts. He's convinced this place is haunted."

She cringed. "I wish he wouldn't say those things. He's always telling our guests about the ghosts. It gives the Luhan House a bad name. He really needs to hold his tongue."

"So you don't believe it—the ghosts?"

She shrugged. "I don't know what to think. You hear the stories, but really? Come on!"

He turned to go and then had second thoughts. "By the way, how long was Kate planning to stay? Her reservation?"

"The whole week. Her reservation runs through Friday. I don't know whether to charge her card or not. The sheriff wants me to keep the room the way she left it, not to touch a thing."

"Tricky," he said, mostly to himself as he walked outside. He sat in one of the chairs on the patio and looked out over the grounds. He had no leads and no cards left to play. Unless he could locate the sixth person at the party.

He cursed out loud. People didn't just fucking disappear without a trace. There had to be an explanation.

While he pondered, he saw the sheriff's car drive into the parking lot and park next to his Cherokee. Hank climbed out of the car and stretched. Another officer, a dog handler, got out of the passenger's seat and walked around to the rear and opened the door. An old bloodhound jumped gingerly out of the back and shook its head, ears flopping. The handler snapped a leash on the dog and the three of them ambled up to the courtyard.

Hank waved. He walked into the office and came out with the key to the Cather Room. "Good! You'll want to come along."

Hank motioned toward the dog. "This here's Bullet, he's the best goddamn bloodhound in the state of New Mexico. He's been known to find a body six years dead and six feet underground. Got a nose like a radar."

The mangy old dog panted and wheezed and slobbered, ignoring the humans gathered around him.

"Took a while to bring him up from Bernalillo County. He's the best, ain't you Bullet?" Hank said, petting the dog.

Fernando almost laughed. "How old is the dog?"

"Don't matter," Hank replied. "What matters is his nose."

Fernando followed them to the Cather Room. Hank opened the door with his key and let the dog in. The dog walked around the room sniffing this, that, and the other. Finally Hank grabbed the slacks Kate had worn and left on the bed. He rubbed the cloth on Bullet's nose and then took him out on the patio. The dog wagged its tail once or twice and then, sniffing the ground, made a beeline toward the gate at the end of the courtyard.

Once through the gate the dog stopped and sniffed the ground again. Then old Bullet headed left on the dirt trail, sniffing his way to the fence where he stopped and looked around. He sniffed left, he sniffed right. He squeezed under the fence and sniffed around the Taos Pueblo land adjoining the Luhan property. He emitted a little sound, more like a whine than a bark, and came back under the fence. He plopped his rear end down on the trail and looked up at Hank. Defeated.

"Well, fuck me! If old Bullet can't find her, she ain't here. Some damn UFO must have beamed her up. I don't know what the hell to think."

Neither did Fernando. Apparently Kate had walked down to the fence and vanished. Into thin air. It didn't make sense.

"What do you want me to do?" the dog handler asked.

Hank threw up his hands. "Take him back down to Bernalillo, I guess. Lotta trouble for nothing."

Hank turned to Fernando. "You're a hotshot from Santa Fe...what do you think?"

"No idea," Fernando said. "I'm just as stumped as you are. I may have to go back to Santa Fe empty handed."

Hank grumbled something to himself and followed the dog and his handler back to the parking lot.

Out of options, Fernando decided to see what he could see on the other side of the fence, Taos Pueblo land. So he found a place to cross and held open the strands of wire, stepping carefully through the strands. Then he walked across the flat mesa, spotted with sage and saltbush and occasional outcroppings of rock. He stopped after about 100 yards. There was nothing out here. It was just empty mesa until you got to the Pueblo or all the way to the mountains. So he turned around and hiked back to the fence.

Hank and the dog team were long gone by the time he reached the parking lot. He spotted Francis watching him from the door of the Luhan House as he climbed into his Cherokee.

He drove back to his room at the El Pueblo and sat in the stuffed chair with his cell phone to look at the photos he took of Kate's portfolio. He read through the pages methodically finding pretty much the same information he'd seen earlier. Most of it was background information on Willa Cather's life, her visits to the Luhan House, and the novels she was working on at the time. Near the end of the portfolio he came across a page of scrawled notes he hadn't noticed, possibly because the handwriting looked rushed and incomprehensible at first glance. The notes mentioned night-time recordings of ghostly voices captured in the Luhan House by the Taos Paranormal Society.

He read: "...mostly female voices...Mabel and Frieda, D.H. Lawrence's...what?...wife?...O'Keefe for sure...and maybe Cather...the one with the plain, sing-song voice...bland, even boring...talking about betrayal...another woman's voice...angry...shouting...a scream!"

He studied the loose handwriting, trying to make sense of the transcription. Betrayal? Of what? While he brooded his eyes grew heavy and he felt his head slowly sinking.

Some time later the vibrations and ring of his cell phone jolted him awake. The phone dropped on the carpet. He reached down and picked up the phone expecting to hear Estelle's voice.

"Detective Lopez? This is Rachel. Are you still in Taos?"

"Uh...yeah," he said, struggling to sit up in the chair, still groggy. He rubbed his eyes, trying to wake up.

After a long silence, Rachel said, "I'm calling to dismiss you."

It took a moment for that to register. "Dismiss me? What do you mean?"

"I mean you can forget about finding Kate. I don't need you any more. I'll pay for whatever expenses you've incurred, but no more."

"I don't understand. Why the change of heart?"

She sighed. "I can't explain. Sorry."

Fernando stood up and began to pace from one end of the room to the other. "Why? What's happened? Are you being threatened?"

"Don't ask, please. I just can't explain."

"But Kate might be in danger," he said. "Her friend Caitlin was murdered at her house Saturday night. Kate was there."

No response.

"Okay, I'm on my way back to Santa Fe. I'm coming to your house for an explanation…to make sure you're okay."

"No! Please…."

The phone went dead.

7

Fernando smelled a rat. Something must have happened to make Rachel change her mind. He intended to find out what. Which meant he would have to drive back to Santa Fe and confront her. First, though, he had to settle up for the room, so he went to the office and asked for his bill. The guy at the front counter looked at him skeptically, an overweight middle-aged man wearing a Mr. Rogers sweater. "But we've already charged you for the night. We can't give you a refund this late in the day. I'm sorry, but that's our policy."

"No problem. I'll pay for tonight...and I might be back tomorrow, I don't know yet."

The clerk ran his credit card and printed out his bill. "Okay, then. Thank you. We hope to see you tomorrow."

He went back to the room and stuffed his shaving kit and loose clothing into his duffel bag. After giving the room a once over, he walked outside and tossed the duffel into the back of the Cherokee. By 7:30 he was heading south on Highway 68 out of Taos. He was tempted to stop at the Taos Grill for a quick dinner, but decided to wait until Española. There were plenty of fast food joints in Española that wouldn't slow him down. He would have to make due with drive-thru food tonight if he wanted to get home at a decent hour. Which he did. He didn't relish the thought of driving seventy, eighty miles in the dark.

Driving through Ranchos de Taos he turned on his headlights. Then he opened his window and let in the cool evening air to keep him awake on the long drive. Meanwhile the sky darkened overhead. The sweeping curves approaching the river forced him to slow down. Because of limited visibility he watched carefully for oncoming traffic. He saw only one vehicle on the highway ahead that roared by and quickly disappeared down the hill toward Taos.

Somewhere before Piedra Lumbre Canyon headlights appeared in his rear view mirror. The headlights quickly grew brighter until the car was right on top of him, tailgating. He slowed down to let the car pass, but the car continued to inch closer, finally bumping against the Cherokee. He hit the accelerator and moved away, only to have the car match his speed and then pull up beside him as if to pass. He turned his head but couldn't get a good look at the two dark figures inside the car, a huge Ford Crown Vic with a loud muffler.

Not knowing what to do, Fernando hit the brakes. The Crown Vic did the same and then veered into his lane, smashing into the front of the Cherokee. He lost control. The Cherokee's right front tire hit the soft shoulder and began to wobble, jolting him. He fought the steering wheel with both hands, bringing the heavy vehicle back onto the highway for only a moment before the Crown Vic smashed into him again, this time with more force.

The Cherokee spun out of control. The vehicle slid sideways on the sandy shoulder, threatening to overturn. He wrenched the steering wheel to the right and managed to turn the vehicle perpendicular to the highway. The Cherokee plunged down the side of a ravine and smacked into its far bank, then rolled back. The impact threw him against the steering wheel, knocking the wind out of him. For a moment he couldn't breathe. His lungs ached for air.

He panicked. Too much adrenaline to feel the pain. He needed to get out of the vehicle fast. He grabbed his Smith & Wessen out of the glove compartment and opened the driver's side door. Crouching low, he moved around to the front of the Cherokee for protection. He saw the Crown Vic stopped a few hundred feet up the highway. Finally it turned around in the middle of the blacktop and then came back slowly, stopping again at the spot where he had veered into the ravine. From that distance the car looked brown—or maybe a dirty red color.

He waited, ready for them if they were foolish enough to walk down the ravine exposed. They weren't. After a few seconds the Crown Vic roared and took off in a sudden burst of acceleration. He listened to the loud muffler grow fainter, making sure they had gone away. Then he took stock of his situation. The left side of the Cherokee was banged up pretty badly, the side mirror missing. He saw nothing that should affect the engine, as far as he could tell in the dark. The rear tires had sunk into loose sand at the bottom of the ravine. Everything else looked fine.

He climbed back in the front seat and started his engine. He placed his weapon in the cubbyhole between seats for quick access. Even with 4-wheel drive, his rear tires spun and kicked up gravel when he put the vehicle in gear. The Cherokee rocked back and forth, but couldn't get out of the sand. So he took the shovel he kept in the back compartment and threw whatever rocks he could find in the ravine under the rear tires. He even found a piece of lumber, which he placed beneath his left rear tire. This time when he fired the engine and hit the accelerator, the Cherokee rocked once and then lurched forward out of the sand, finding firmer ground.

He turned his lights on for a moment, just to get the lay of the land. Up ahead the ravine wasn't as deep. He thought he could drive up over the lip of the ravine onto the highway. Using only his safety lights, he drove slowly to the spot he wanted and then gunned the engine. The Cherokee sputtered, kicking up dirt and gravel as the tires dug into the embankment. Finally the vehicle lurched over the lip and skidded onto the blacktop. Once there, he turned his lights back on and drove down to the Rio Grande Gorge Visitor Center, which had already closed for the night. He pulled into the driveway and parked behind the center where the Cherokee couldn't be seen from the dark highway.

Then he turned the motor off and waited. Everything quieted down except for an occasional vehicle passing by on the highway. None stopped or slowed down.

Safe for the moment, he brooded on his next move. Rachel and now apparently someone in Taos wanted him off the Kate Isaacs case bad enough to try and kill him. Or maybe it was the Caitlin Adams case. Or both.

The immediate question was whether to continue on to Santa Fe or remain in Taos. If he left for Santa Fe now, he wouldn't arrive until nearly Midnight, too late to call on Rachel. If he stayed in Taos, he could go back to the El Pueblo and claim his room, a room he'd already paid for tonight. Finally he decided staying in Taos was the smart thing to do. He could start fresh tomorrow morning.

Fernando drove around the visitor center to the highway and stopped to look around. No sign of the Crown Vic or any other traffic. So he eased out onto the highway and drove back into Taos. When he turned into the El Pueblo he pulled up in front of his room at the end of the motel. The same fifty-something guy in the Mr. Rogers sweater greeted him at the front counter.

"Welcome back. I didn't think I'd see you this soon."

"Neither did I. Can I have my keycard back?"

The clerk handed him the card. "You want to start a new tab?"

'Why not," he said. "I may never leave."

The clerk smiled slightly, the first time Fernando had seen the man express any emotion.

He took his duffel bag and Smith & Wessen out of the Cherokee and walked into his room. The room hadn't been touched since he left. The bed wasn't made and the coffee machine hadn't been refreshed. That reminded him that he hadn't eaten all day, so he strapped on his concealed carry holster, deposited the gun, and then walked down to Michael's Kitchen for yet another Enchilada plate and Modelo.

By the time he'd finished his meal he'd gone through a second Modelo and was feeling no pain. He checked his phone and found two texts, one from Estelle and another from Rachel.

"Why don't you call me?" Estelle wrote.

"I meant what I said today. Please stop the investigation," Rachel wrote.

He ignored Rachel's text. He would deal with that tomorrow.

Estelle he couldn't put off. So he bit the bullet and called her, apologizing for not calling earlier. He told her about his efforts to find the missing woman but left out his run-in (literally) with the Crown Vic. No need to upset her.

"Well, I don't understand," she said finally. "You're supposed to be retired. Why can't you stay in town and just do divorce cases. Stuff like that?"

With that he promised to call tomorrow.

Divorce cases? He wondered if she were trying to tell him something.

8

Fernando awoke to a pounding on his door. He checked the time. Nearly nine o'clock. He hadn't slept that late in years. Must have been tired.

He scrambled to find his pants and then hobbled to the door. "Who's there?"

"Housekeeping," he heard in response.

Though the peephole he saw a young woman standing in front of a cart overflowing with linens. He opened the door a crack and waved at the mess in his room. "Forget about it. I don't need anything at the moment."

She moved to the side and looked around him at the mess. "You sure?"

"I'm good," he said and shut the door.

He walked barefoot into the bathroom and splashed water on his face, trying to avoid the image in the mirror, the wrinkled brown face and the bags under his eyes. He kept his salt and pepper hair short, because short there seemed to be more pepper than salt. He hated to look at his reflection. He just didn't feel as old as he looked. Normally. Although today, with ribs bruised from slamming against his steering wheel, he felt about as bad as he looked.

He brushed his teeth and combed his thinning hair. Then he put on a clean shirt from his duffel bag and sat down in the chair to think. Coffee. He needed coffee, so he went over to the automatic coffee maker on the bathroom counter and rummaged through yesterday morning's coffee mess. Under a pile of wrappers and used napkins he found one unused coffee pod and brewed himself a fast cup. He'd just sat back down in his chair when his cell phone buzzed and then rang.

"Howdy Fernando!" boomed the now familiar voice. "You still in Taos?"

He laughed. "Looks like I may never get out of here."

"Good, because this Kate Isaacs woman is fixin' to drive me crazy."

"What now?"

"Come on over to the Luhan House and see for yourself," Hank said and clicked off.

Now what? He wished Hank would take the time to explain himself. The man always seemed to be in a hurry.

He drank his coffee and then finished dressing. No time for breakfast now, so he strapped on his holster and walked out to the Cherokee. He put the do-not-disturb card on the doorknob outside, since he had no idea when he would be back or even if he would be spending another night. The uncertainty was starting to piss him off. He didn't like uncertainty.

In the daylight the Cherokee didn't look as bad as it did last night. The front fender would have to be replaced, as well as the missing mirror. Probably the front bumper too, since it was bent perilously close to the left front tire.

Traffic was light on the way to the Luhan House. Took him no more than a couple minutes. He turned left on Morada and then into the Luhan House parking lot. He saw Hank standing next to his cruiser. Several people gathered around him, including Francis from the office and Tom, who sat in the ATV used by the groundskeepers. One other individual stood off to the side. He wore a running suit and looked like a guest on his morning walk.

They all stared at Fernando as he stepped out of the Cherokee and came over to join them. Hank opened his arms wide and said, "You see what I mean?"

"See what?"

"Her car's gone. She came back to get her car. Or somebody did."

Only then did Fernando notice the absence of the blue Passat. He shook his head, not understanding.

He turned to Francis. "Did she stop by the office?"

"No. No one saw her. She must have come after hours."

"Did she take any of her belongings from the room?"

"No. The room hasn't been touched. We called her partner, Rachel, in Santa Fe. She's coming up this afternoon to pick up Kate's belongings. Hank said it would be okay."

Fernando nodded. "Then I'll stop by later."

Hank removed his Stetson and scratched his head. "What I want to know is what in the hell is going on here? Why would she disappear in the middle of the night and then come back for her car again in the middle of the night? It doesn't make any damn sense!"

Hank looked accusingly at Francis first and then at Fernando. Neither of them spoke.

Tom broke the silence. "Nah, she's probably just visiting friends up here. No need to get all worked up about it. Someone picked her up and then brought her back to get her car."

Hank frowned but held his tongue.

Francis stared at Tom for a moment and then nodded. "Maybe," she said, heading back to the office followed by the guest in the running suit.

"Okay then." Tom waved and drove off in his ATV all smiles, like everything had just been settled.

Hank turned to him. "I don't like it. Something's wrong."

"You don't know the half of it."

"Maybe I don't want to know the other half," Hank said. Then he noticed the damage to Fernando's Cherokee. "Whoa Nellie, what happened there? You get in an accident last night?"

"That's the other half I'm talking about," Fernando said.

"Well, hell...I haven't had breakfast yet. Have you? I could eat a horse."

"You're on. Michael's?"

"I'll meet you there."

He followed Hank back to Paseo del Pueblo Norte and into the parking lot beside Michael's Kitchen. "I don't know what I would do without this place," Hank said, coming over to him in the parking lot. "I just might starve to death. Since my wife died, I have to cook for myself. And I'm one sorry ass cook."

All the servers in Michael's knew Hank. They swarmed around him like bees to honey as soon as they stepped inside. Hank spotted his favorite, an older woman named Stella, and she showed them to a corner table. Hank removed his Stetson and placed it on an extra chair.

"What can I get you fellers?" Stella asked, a tiny woman with a long gray hair wearing jeans and a man's western shirt.

They both ordered huevos rancheros and coffee. "Thank you darling," Hank said as Stella headed for he kitchen.

Then Hank leaned back in his chair and sighed. "Tell me, Fernando, why in hell did you decide to get back in the game? When I retire I'm for damn sure not going to go private."

Fernando laughed. "After this, I might reconsider."

"So what happened last night?" Hank asked, getting serious.

"Long story. I got a call from Rachel Wolfe, Kate's partner, telling me to stop the search and drop the case. I asked why, but she said she couldn't say. And she sounded upset. So last night after dark I decided to return to Santa Fe and confront her. Find out what's going on. I got about as far as the Gorge Visitor Center when this Ford Crown Vic came up behind me and started ramming my Cherokee. It looked like two guys in the front seat, I didn't get a good look at them. Bastards ran me off the highway into a ravine and left me there."

"Sounds like they wanted to scare you off."

"I'd say they did a pretty good job."

"Crown Vic, you say? What color?"

"It looked brown or maybe red," Fernando said. "I couldn't tell for sure in the dark."

"Hmmm...seems to me my deputy had a run-in with some clown driving a Crown Vic a year or so ago. I can't remember the details. Let me check and get back to you."

"What about the Caitlin Adams investigation? Anything new there?"

Hank shook his head. "Not much so far. Forensics is still trying to match fingerprints and DNA. They've identified the DNA of two of the people at the party, the Baca twins. We're trying to get samples from Billy Jackson and the neighbor, Mark Roybal. Mark and Caitlin had been feuding for years. Calling in complaints about each other. So far Mark has refused, so we're getting a court order requiring him to comply. We'll see."

"What about this sixth person at the party?"

"You tell me. At the moment Kate and number six are our main suspects. We were hoping you'd help us out by finding Kate. I get the feeling that wherever Kate is, number six won't be far away."

"And neither will the blue Passat," Fernando said.

Just then Stella arrived with their plates and a bottle of ketchup for Hank. "You boys let me know if you need anything else. Your coffee is on its way."

"Much obliged," Hank said, tucking his napkin in the neck of his shirt and reaching for the ketchup.

Fernando watched Hank smother his plate of huevos rancheros in ketchup.

Hank looked at Fernando. "What? You don't use ketchup?"

"Not on huevos rancheros."

Hank smiled. "It's an acquired taste."

9

Fernando recognized Rachel's BMW as he pulled into the Luhan House parking lot. It was the same red Beamer he'd seen outside his office window Monday morning when his troubles started.

He parked next to the BMW and climbed out of his Cherokee. Going up the steps he saw her standing up on the flagstone porch talking to Francis, a large canvas tote back at her feet. She looked even paler outside in the sun than she did inside, with her face as white as death and ringed by fiery red hair streaked with blue. When she saw him approaching, she turned her head and said something to Francis. Then she took the tote bag and hurried down to the Cather Room.

He nodded to Francis, who looked away, and followed Rachel to the Cather Room. She shut the door in his face as he tried to enter. Without a word.

He knocked, waiting. Finally the door opened a crack and she said, "I told you I didn't need your services any more. Now please leave me alone!"

She tried to close the door, but he pushed it open and stepped inside.

"Please! Go away!" she said.

"Not until you tell me why you changed your mind."

"I can't! I've already told you! I can't say any more than I have!"

"Why? Have you heard from Kate?"

"No! Not exactly! Please!"

He noticed her entire body shaking. She was that upset.

She put her hands over her face and sat down on the nearest bed. "I can't do this!"

"Is Kate in hiding?" Fernando asked. "Like I told you before, her friend Caitlin was murdered Saturday night and she's one of the suspects. Is that why she disappeared?"

"No!"

"Has she been kidnapped?"

When she didn't respond, he finally understood.

After a long silence he said, "Why don't you tell me about it?"

She sighed but didn't speak.

"Have you gone to the police yet?" he asked.

"No! I can't! They said they'd kill her if I went to the police. They want two hundred and fifty thousand dollars by Saturday. Or I'll never see her again."

He shook his head. A ransom of two hundred fifty thousand dollars was not much of a ransom. That told him they were dealing with a bunch of amateurs. Which meant they were inexperienced. Which in turn meant they were unpredictable. Dangerously unpredictable.

'That's a strange amount to ask for," he said.

"I know it's not a lot of money...."

"Well, it is if you have to raise it quickly," he said.

"Exactly. I think I can have it by this Saturday, but it won't be easy. We have most of our money invested in the Tesuque house. I'll have to get a second mortgage...take out some cash."

He nodded. "What instructions did they give you?"

"They told me to get the money and wait for them to contact me."

He walked across the room and sat on the bed beside her. "Listen, Rachel. This is dangerous business. If you're not going to call the police, then at least let me help you. You'll need an intermediary, someone to go back and forth. Someone to protect you and to make sure Kate is still alive. Do you understand?"

She nodded but said nothing.

He looked around the room. "Are you going back to Santa Fe tonight?"

"Yes, as soon as I finish here. Shouldn't take long."

"Okay, I'll be at home or in my office on Canyon Road. As soon as you hear from them, call me. Try to put them off for a day or two. Tell them you're still raising the money. That'll give me some time to investigate."

"It's true, I will need some time to raise the money. I have a ten o'clock appointment at our bank tomorrow morning."

He stood up to go. "Remember, call me as soon as you hear from them. Or sooner if something else happens."

With that he stepped out of the room and walked across the courtyard. Tom waved cheerfully from over by the Pink House where he was cutting back the shrubbery threatening to engulf the derelict building. Silent Jim sat on the sagging porch watching the younger man work.

Fernando waved back as he climbed into the Cherokee and fired the big engine. He drove back around to the El Pueblo and checked out. Again.

The old guy with the Mr. Rogers sweater smiled as he handed him the receipt. "Be back later today?"

"Not today. Maybe tomorrow."

"See you tomorrow," Mr. Rogers said.

He took his time driving out of Taos, enjoying the bright spring day. No need to worry about the Crown Vic in the daylight. Cowards worked at night. He relaxed as he drove by Pilar, noticing the rafts and kayaks bobbing in the white water rapids of the Rio Grande.

The long drive to Santa Fe gave him time to think. Things began to make sense. The two men in the Crown Vic were working with the kidnappers. So, too, was the sixth person at the party Saturday. In fact, number six probably killed Caitlin.

He decided to honor Rachel's wish and not tell Hank about the kidnapping. Better to keep the sheriff's office out of the loop, at least for the moment. Hank would find out soon enough.

So everything fell on him. He had to find the kidnappers and free Kate—safely. And he had to do it by Saturday. So much for being retired.

10

Estelle chastised Fernando as soon as he walked into their house on Acequia Madre. Predictably, she said, "Why didn't you call, I've been worried sick!" And then she gave him a big hug. She never stayed mad for long. They were still affectionate after thirty years of marriage, inseparable really, except when he had to work. They had come a long way together, he and Estelle. They were just kids when they married: he a young twenty and Estelle all of nineteen.

For the first few years of their marriage he worked part-time at Johnson's Lumber Yard and took classes at UNM, majoring in Criminal Justice. When Flavia was born, their first child, he dropped out of UNM and entered the Santa Fe Police Academy. Not only did he need a full-time job to support the family, he decided that instead of studying Criminal Justice he would rather work in the field.

Those early years in the SFPD were the hardest because of the way he and the other young Chicanos were treated. It didn't matter that his mother was an Anglo; his last name always dictated the way he was perceived by his superiors. But he had a mortgage to pay and a family to raise, so he stuck it out and tried not to let the insults bother him even though they did. He internalized his anger and used it as motivation. He endured, outlasting the bastards and rising through the ranks until he reached his final position as senior detective.

Early on Estelle feared for his safety every day when he left for the station, but over the years she seemed to accept the risks involved. She knew he was a careful, conscientious man who did not like to take chances. She learned to trust him, and he in turn learned to accommodate her need to be kept informed about his whereabouts and his safety. He tried to accommodate her need, anyway.

When he retired last year after his final blow-out with the Chief, he told himself he would take it easy and live a quiet, stress-free life. That lasted for about three months.

He tried his best to relax and settle into retirement, puttering around the house and garden, but something was missing. He hated to admit it, but he missed his work. Not his job, because there he had to put up with the Chief and the other arrogant city officials, all of them younger than him and not half as steeped in Santa Fe history. He missed the work: the people, the investigations, the adrenaline rushes. He happened to believe that criminals and scumbags should be off the streets. Becoming a private investigator allowed him to continue his work—without the job.

Estelle had dinner waiting inside, a welcome home dinner of his favorite meal: red chile enchiladas with posole followed by mocha cake from an old family recipe. He always felt a sense of relief when he stepped inside their small adobe, where they had lived since they were first married. Stress from work seemed to melt away the instant he walked into the snug, comfortable spaces of their home. The house might be small by today's standards, but it had been big enough to raise two children back in his day, before the rich Anglos from New York and Los Angeles moved into Santa Fe and remodeled the old adobes on streets like Acequia Madre into ten and twenty room mansions.

He took great pride in the fact that he had preserved the original look of his simple adobe, built in the 1920s. He couldn't care less that their house had become something of an eyesore to the Sotheby crowd. Anyway, the crumbling adobe wall around their house and back patio prevented the nouveau Santa Feans from bothering them.

Estelle loved the color blue, so they had painted their front door and windows blue, which according to tradition kept evil spirits from entering the house. Not stopping there, Estelle hand painted their kitchen cupboards the same turquoise blue color. So far it had worked like a charm. He didn't really consider himself a superstitious man, but then again he didn't really disbelieve in superstitions either. Many of them were traditions that ran deep in the culture, so deep they were a part of everyday life, a part of who they were, call them what you will.

After dinner they had tea on their back patio. Estelle told him about her work at the Saint Francis Outreach Program. The nonprofit provided food and clothing to the growing immigrant community in Santa Fe, a sanctuary city. He told her about his latest case—the missing woman who turned out to be kidnapped, and the murder of a friend of the missing woman, which may or may not be connected to the kidnapping. He didn't tell her about the Crown Vic incident and the damage to his new Cherokee. He'd parked the Cherokee off to the side of their garage, not directly behind her car, hoping she wouldn't notice the banged up Cherokee. He hoped to take it to an auto body repair shop in next few days.

Eventually Estelle went inside to get ready for bed. He stayed on the patio for a few more minutes thinking about Kate Isaacs. There was nothing to do now but wait for the kidnappers to call. When they did he had absolutely no idea about what he was going to do.

11

After breakfast Fernando helped Estelle get off to work, carrying boxes of donated clothing out to her Camry. Trying to keep her away from his Cherokee so she wouldn't notice the damage. Today she and her co-workers were collecting clothing for the immigrant community in Santa Fe, most of whom were passing through to larger cities in Colorado or Texas. None of them could afford to live in Santa Fe. People who lived in Santa Fe couldn't even afford to live in Santa Fe. Thanks to gentrification.

When he walked back into the house his cell phone was ringing on the counter.

He expected to hear Hank's voice, but instead it was a woman's.

"Detective Lopez, it's Rachel...they called."

"They? You mean the kidnappers?"

"Yes, I when I got back from jogging this morning I found a message on my machine. They said they would call back at Noon to give me instructions about where to meet them with the money. I thought you might want to be there when they call, if you think...."

"I would, yes. Where in Tesuque do you live?"

She gave him her address on Bishop's Lodge Road and directions.

"Okay, I'll be there at eleven thirty."

She clicked off without responding.

He brewed himself another cup of coffee and took it out on the patio. Something about Rachel put him off. Her evasiveness, her reluctance to open up. Even though she'd come to him for help, she seemed hesitant to provide him with the information he needed. He prided himself on being able to read people, but Rachel remained a mystery to him.

While waiting for the Noon phone call, he drove down to his office and checked the machine for messages. Nada.

A few minutes later he heard a vehicle pull into the gravel parking lot outside. Through the window he saw Ruby's Honda Accord. She parked the Accord next to his Cherokee and slammed the door a couple of times to get it closed. Ruby looked absolutely radiant today, not her usual pottery studio grunge with her face and work clothes smudged with brown clay. Today she wore slacks and a black silk shirt with a turquoise necklace hanging between her breasts. All business.

"Wow!" he said, stepping out of his office. "You look hot! If I wasn't a married man, I'd ask you out."

Ruby spied him walking up to the parking lot. "Hah! Like I've said a million times, I've had three husbands already and I'm not looking for number four! Not even you, Fernando!"

He and Ruby had known each other since their days at Santa Fe High. They shared the same politics and the same bad attitude. He tried to keep his negativity under wraps, but Ruby wore her bad attitude with pride. To her, it was a badge of honor. Her in-your-face personality put off many people but had made her a force in Santa Fe politics for over two decades. A potter by trade, Ruby had risen through the ranks of *La Raza* to become the most progressive member of City Council ever. Back in the 1990s she fought tooth and nail with all the greedy developers who wanted to turn downtown Santa Fe into one big shopping mall. She led rallies, marches, protests, sit-ins, and if you believed the rumors, a fire-bombing or two.

She lost, of course. The developers and the Sotheby's crowd turned Santa Fe into Disneyland Southwest. The tide of gentrification sweeping over Santa Fe during those years hollowed out the city. Gone were most of the people whose families had lived in Santa Fe for generations. Ever higher home values and property taxes priced out all who couldn't afford million dollar homes. After two tumultuous terms on City Council lecturing, berating, cajoling, and threatening the other members, she said 'fuck it' and retired to the pottery co-op she owned and ran with a number of other potters, most of them women.

Still, Ruby refused to be silenced. She made it a point to attend most Council meetings and give the members a piece of her mind. Every one of them feared Ruby's tirades. Occasionally her anger would get the better of her language and she would be asked to leave. Once a few years back City Council banned her for the year, but her lawyer, Raoul Garcia, sued their asses and got Ruby reinstated in her front row seat staring down the Council.

Ruby was a Santa Fe legend. The real thing. He loved her.

"You opening the gallery today?" he asked.

"Yeah, now that the tourists season has started. We'll see who wanders in off Canyon Road. What about you? Have you had any business yet?"

He told her about Rachel hiring him to find her husband, Kate Isaacs, who'd gone missing and apparently kidnapped.

"No kidding? Someone kidnapped that bitch? Hard to believe."

"What do you mean?"

Ruby looked at him. "Have you met her?"

"No, only Rachel. Who wasn't that damn friendly."

"I'm not surprised. They're militant lesbians, both of them. I know a lot of lesbians, but I don't know any who hate men as much as Kate. If she has been kidnapped, I imagine she's giving her kidnappers a hard time. She's a tiger."

"Thanks for the warning."

"Come on in, I'll show you what I've done to the gallery."

He followed her inside for a quick tour. She'd totally redone the inside of the building, an old carriage house, since inheriting the property from husband number three Jimmy Mackey. She kept some of Jimmy's paintings hanging on the walls, including two of his infamous "Chopped Nudes" series, which showed female body parts arranged in weird ways. The counters and shelves displayed ceramics made by the women at her pottery co-op.

After the tour she turned to him and said, "Hey—stop by later. We'll go over to El Farol for a drink."

"You talked me into it," he said, returning to his office.

A short time later he left for Tesuque. He drove down to the Paseo and around to Bishop's Lodge Road. The two-lane took him past Fort Marcy Park and the road to the Ski Basin. He passed by the site of Bishop's Lodge, originally built by Archbishop Lamy in the 19th century and now the location of a fancy Santa Fe resort for wealthy tourists. Around the last bend he entered a scattering of houses that marked the outskirts of the village of Tesuque.

He found the house set back from the road behind a stand of trees. He turned into the driveway and pulled up behind Rachel's BMW. The fact that she drove a Beamer and lived in Tesuque, where the price of houses started at a cool million, told him she could raise the ransom money without much sweat. He parked the Cherokee and followed a sidewalk that took him between the garage on the right and a guesthouse on the left. The guesthouse had been converted to a studio for Kate's podcasts. Through a window in the door he noticed a Rode Podcaster and professional mixer placed on a long table, along with computers and four microphones and chairs. Professional lights and a cabinet filled with electronics stood against the rear wall. It looked to him like a professional operation.

He followed the sidewalk to the main building, a frame house with cedar siding and lots of windows. When he knocked, he saw Rachel come to the side window and peer out at him. Then she came to the door and opened it, almost begrudgingly. He felt like asking her if she wanted him to leave but held his tongue.

"This way," she said, leading him into a spacious back room that served as a study and sitting room. The rear wall was a row of windows with French doors opening on to a patio. The windows looked out on Tesuque's receding hills, red triangles dotted with green piñon and juniper trees. The other walls of the room were decorated with bright modernist paintings that looked expensive. In fact, everything here looked expensive.

"Nice place," Fernando said.

Rachel ignored him.

"How do you want to do this?"

She pointed to a leather chair beside a corner table on which the phone rested. He did as he was directed and sat in the chair.

She stared at him, as if deciding what to do next. "Can I get you something? Tea? Coffee?"

'No thanks, I'm good."

So she sat down in a leather chair on the opposite side of the corner table. They waited in silence for a good ten minutes, both staring at the phone.

When finally the phone rang both of them jumped.

She picked up the receiver and said, "Yes?"

Fernando heard a muffled voice. The caller sounded like someone speaking through a handkerchief, someone whose voice was vaguely familiar. He listened closely, managing to pick up occasional words and phrases: "two hundred fifty thousand dollars...in small bills...tens and twenties...come alone...noon...behind the Blake Hotel...at the ski basin... alone." The caller ended by screaming: "Or your friend is dead!"

He knew that voice from somewhere. Then it clicked. He'd heard it at the Luhan House in Taos. Tom, the groundskeeper. He was almost certain. The sonofabitch must be working with the kidnappers.

Rachel put down the receiver, her hands shaking. "What do you think?"

"I think I recognize the voice."

She stared at him.

"One thing I do know. Two hundred fifty thousand dollars in tens and twenties is a lot of bills. Transporting that amount won't be easy—for you or them."

"What about the voice?"

Fernando shook his head. "I don't want to incriminate anyone until I'm sure. I'll need to go back to Taos. We don't have much time. Are you prepared to meet them on Saturday, with or without the money?"

She nodded tentatively. "I guess...."

"Then you can get the money?"

She nodded.

"Okay then, I'll call you from Taos when I have a plan. Be ready!"

She accompanied him to the front door, locking it behind him. He climbed into the Cherokee and headed back to Santa Fe, already making plans to stop by the house for his duffel bag. He should be in Taos by two o'clock. if he hurried. Time was short.

Ruby would have to wait for that drink at El Farol.

12

Driving through Pilar Fernando slowed down to watch the rafts and kayaks bounce down the white water rapids of the Rio Grande. He didn't see Billy Jackson's pickup or Great River Rafting Adventures's trailer, but there were plenty of other rafting company trucks parked in the lot or on the shoulder of the highway. Congested, as it always was from April through October.

He drove into Taos to Kit Carson Road and then turned left onto Morada. He wanted to speak with Francis first, before he made a decision about how to proceed. So he parked in the lot and made his way up to the office, where she stood behind the front desk talking to an elderly male guest. She gave the guest directions to the Taos Pueblo and then handed him a brochure.

"It's well worth the trip," Francis said. "The five-story pueblo is one thousand years old. A World Heritage site."

"Thanks," the man said and walked away.

Fernando waited his turn and then approached.

"Back again, I see," she said, looking as stately as ever in a maroon suit and pink scarf.

"Yes, for the moment. I wanted to ask you about Tom."

"Tom? What about?"

"What do you know about him? In particular, do you know if he's ever been in trouble with the law?"

She looked surprised. "Well, he's only worked here for a couple of years. I don't really know that much about him. We've never had a problem with him, if that's what you mean. He does what he's asked to do. Always been a good worker."

"He's never been in legal trouble?"

"Not as far as I know. Why? Is he in some kind of trouble now?"

"I don't know. Maybe."

She frowned.

"When does he get off work?"

"Five o'clock...unless he's in the middle of finishing a job," she said. "You can tell if he's here by looking for his Jeep. He parks it over by the maintenance building on the far side of the parking lot."

"Okay, thanks."

He hadn't noticed the Jeep parked on the side of the maintenance building, but he saw it now as he walked into the parking lot. An older model orange Wrangler that looked like it had seen better days, partially hidden by a wooden fence. Now that he knew what Tom was driving, he climbed back into the Cherokee and drove to the end of Morada Road, pulling over behind a bank of garbage cans. From here he had a clear view of vehicles coming and going from the Luhan House parking lot. All he had to do was wait.

He entertained himself by googling Tom Jensen with his cell phone but found no listing, address or telephone number, for a Tom Jensen living in Taos. After about an hour he started getting restless. Five o'clock was still an hour away. He suffered through another half hour before he saw a welcome sight: the orange Wrangler pulling out of the parking lot and heading for Kit Carson Road.

He eased around the garbage cans and followed. The Jeep turned right on Kit Carson and right again on Paseo del Pueblo Norte. Traffic was backed up on the Paseo, too many tourists arriving in town at the end of the day, so he found himself several vehicles behind the Wrangler by the time he managed to turn onto the Paseo. Still, he could see the bright orange Jeep up ahead since everyone was moving slowly on the two-lane road.

The line of cars started to thin out as the newcomers reached their hotels and other destinations. By the time they passed the turn-off to Taos Pueblo he found himself directly behind the Wrangler, so he slowed down to keep his distance. Just before Orlando's Restaurant the Jeep turned into the parking lot of the Red Dog Brewery, an L-shaped frame building with a wooden patio out front where several people were drinking beer. He slowed to a stop and pulled into the Burger King lot next door, parking in the northwest corner of the lot where he had a clear view of the brewery. Then he cut his engine and watched.

Tom stepped out of the Jeep holding a cell phone. His gray ponytail hung loose behind him. He walked up to Red Dog's patio still speaking on the phone and took a seat at one of the tables in the rear. When the server appeared, Tom put away his phone and ordered. Moments later the server returned with a foaming pint of beer. Tom said something to the server and raised his glass. The server, a young woman, laughed and walked away.

Fernando watched Tom drink his first pint of beer and order another. Just as the server brought the second pint a car pulled into the Red Dog lot and parked next to the Wrangler. He smiled when he saw the car, an enormous Crown Vic with so much dust on its fenders that the red paint looked brown. Two men wearing baseball caps hopped out of the Ford and walked up to the patio. He wasn't at all surprised when they approached Tom's table. The two men looked Tom's age, maybe mid forties. One wore fatigues, a tall scruffy looking dude who seemed to be in charge. He barked orders to the small round fellow in denim who followed, ambling along behind. Even from this distance Fernando was certain they were the two sonofabitches who ran him off the road near Pilar.

Fernando watched the two latecomers from the Crown Vic take a seat at the table. When the server appeared, the tall scruffy fellow placed their order. The server brought two more pints and then the three conspirators talked quietly and drank their beers. When they finished the first round, they ordered another. Finally, about seven o'clock, the two men in the Crown Vic paid their bill and left. Laughing, they walked down to the Crown Vic and drove off fast, cutting in and out of traffic. That left Tom alone at the table. He called for the server and ordered food. Minutes later the server brought him a hamburger plate and a small tray of condiments. Again Tom said something that made the server laugh.

Fernando hadn't realized how hungry he was until he watched Tom wolf down his burger. When was the last time he'd eaten? He must have eaten something this morning, but he couldn't remember what. He was starving.

Once finished, Tom left money on the table and walked to his Jeep without looking around, unsuspecting that he was being followed.

Then they were off again, the Jeep in front and the Cherokee keeping its distance. He guessed Tom lived in Arroyo Seco, famous for its collection of old hippies left over from Taos' counterculture past. He wasn't disappointed. Just as he expected the Wrangler turned right on Highway 522 and then again on 230 into the tiny village of Arroyo Seco.

Fernando followed the Jeep into a canyon on the far side of Arroyo Seco. Scrub piñon and juniper trees grew wild on either side of the dirt road. He slowed down over the rough terrain, easing around a long curve. Up ahead he saw the Wrangler pull up in front of an ancient Airstream mobile home, its unpainted aluminum faded and rusted in patches. The Airstream sagged at the front end where the hitch was propped up by cement blocks. Trash of one kind or another littered the ground around the Airstream, which looked like it had been here for a long time. He couldn't imagine it being road-worthy.

He backtracked to an even rougher side road that took him behind an outcropping of rock. He made sure to park where he would not be visible from the road and then took his binoculars out of the glove compartment and hiked to the top of the ridge. From there he had a clear view of the Airstream. He settled in behind a cone-shaped hoodoo and trained his binoculars on the mobile home. Through the open door and the row of windows in front he watched Tom move around inside the Airstream. No one else appeared.

By now light had drained from the Western sky. Soon it would be totally dark. He decided to come back tomorrow while Tom was at work. That way he could take a closer look at the trailer—and what was inside.

He didn't have much time. Rachel was supposed to deliver the money on Saturday, the day after tomorrow. He would have to work fast.

He climbed down to the Cherokee and drove back to Taos, wishing he had a plan. At the El Pueblo the man wearing the Mr. Rogers sweater laughed as he walked into the office. "You know...you might be better off with the weekly rate."

He laughed too. "I think you might be right. At least book me though tomorrow."

"Just one more night? That won't save you any money. Buy hey, it's your dime."

13

Friday morning Fernando took his time. He ate a leisurely breakfast at Michael's Kitchen and then drove over to the Luhan House to make sure Tom was there. Sure enough, he found the orange Wrangler parked in the same spot next to the maintenance building. So he headed out to Arroyo Seco, following the same route he'd taken yesterday. When he turned off on the dirt road to the Airstream he slowed to a crawl, wanting to make sure the mobile home was in fact deserted.

He saw no other vehicles as he rounded the last curve, so he drove over and parked in front of the mobile home. He walked to the two-step wooden porch and tried the door. Locked. So he took out his pocket lock pick and helped himself. Inside the small Airstream he found what he expected in Tom's bachelor pad: a mess. Dirty dishes, dirty clothes, piles of junk packed tightly in close quarters. He stepped carefully through the squalor and examined the tiny bedroom in back first. On a bureau he found a half-used roll of duct tape and a pair of scissors. Underneath the duct tape was a long cotton cloth, torn or cut from a towel. Nothing else on the bed or in the closet drew his attention, so he returned to the front kitchen and sitting area where he again found nothing other than old newspapers, paperbacks and food containers. It looked like Tom lived on fast food. There was no evidence of cooking on the filthy propane stove. The guy was a damned pig.

He smelled smoke when he stepped outside and locked the door behind him. The smoke seemed to be coming from behind the Airstream, so he walked around back and found a smoldering fifty-gallon drum used to burn trash. Inside the drum he spotted everything from burned wood to melted plastic and blackened metal. It was a typical way of disposing trash out in rural communities. Problem was, half the stuff they threw in the drums wouldn't burn, so eventually they had to haul the whole mess away. Most of it ended up illegally dumped along the county roads.

Nothing Fernando could do about that. He shrugged and made his way back to the Cherokee. He started down the dirt road to the highway but stopped just around the long curve, where he pulled over and switched off the engine. He had no idea of what to do next. The duct tape he found in the Airstream could have been used in the kidnapping, but so what? Clearly Kate wasn't being held captive in the damn trailer. So where did that leave him? For lack of a better plan he decided to stop at the Sheriff's office on Lovato Place and talk to Hank. Rachel had asked him not to go to the police, but what choice did he have? Noon Saturday was only twenty-four hours away.

Pondering, he watched the traffic speed by on the highway. Before long he heard the deep roar of a bad muffler approaching. When he looked down the highway he saw a Crown Vic, red but covered in dust and caked mud. He recognized it instantly as the same car that had driven him off the highway and that he had seen at the Red Dog Brewery. He fired the engine and pulled out on the highway following at a safe distance. On the far side of Arroyo Seco the Ford continued on Highway 150, the road to the Taos Ski Basin.

They drove though a long valley of rolling hills and grassland overlaid by a grid of fences that marked the boundaries of small farms and ranches in the valley. Then they entered the foothills climbing into the Carson National Forest. Finally he saw the Crown Vic slow down ahead and turn into a driveway overgrown with weeds. The driveway led to a dilapidated A-frame isolated in the woods. The unpainted structure looked like it could collapse at any moment. Black mold and wood rot were eating their way up the wooden siding from the moist forest floor. The second floor balcony sagged at one end, threatening to fall off. Heavy curtains blocked the dark windows.

Driving by he noticed a row of hand-painted signs warning visitors to stay away: "Keep Out"..."No Trespassing"..."Don't Tread on Me"..."We Shoot to Kill"..."Beware Dog," with "Dog" crossed out and "Demon" painted above. Other signs included symbols as well as crude skull and cross-bones paintings in blood red paint on weathered gray plywood. The largest of the signs was a square panel of plywood painted black and red: a pentangle with a red satanic figure bursting out of its center. A real friendly place.

He continued on for a couple of hundred yards until he spotted a forest road off to the left. Slowing down he turned onto the forest road and parked behind a small ridge covered with piñon and juniper trees. He waited a few minutes to make sure the two guys in the Crown Vic hadn't noticed him and followed. Then he took his holster and binoculars out of the glove compartment and walked into the thick trees. He found what looked like a much-used animal trail littered with scat and followed it back toward the A-frame.

The trail took him down the hill toward a small rise. Next to the trail a gigantic ponderosa pine towered over the rise. Cresting the rise he walked smack dab into the carcass of a dead raccoon hanging by twine from a branch of the ponderosa. He jumped to the side, ducking. The rotting smell of the carcass was enough to make him retch. He spit, wondering what sick fuck would hang a dead coon over a hiking trail. He walked more carefully now, spooked by the dead animal. Was it an omen? Another warning?

He crept forward, moving more cautiously over the dirt and pine needle floor. The trail eventually circled around behind the A-frame to a boulder half-buried in the hillside. He crept down to the boulder and set up with his binoculars, scanning the house and surrounding grounds. From the rear the ramshackle house looked even worse. Its entire left side seemed to sag into the ground. Patches of dry rot discolored most of its wood siding, while above on its roof several shingles hung loose or had fallen off completely. The screen door in back hung open, its screen ripped.

The grounds were just as bad. A line of rusted and abandoned vehicles provided a barrier of sorts between the property and the forest, while directly behind the A-frame a trash dump had been dug and filled with discarded appliances including a stove and a portable television. Further back he saw another wooden building, a small barn or maybe a tool shed. To either side of the shed bullet-riddled targets had been nailed to the ponderosa pines and used for target practice.

Finally he focused his binoculars on the A-frame. Through its back window he could see two people arguing in what appeared to be a kitchen. The taller of the two yelled and then shoved the shorter one, who slunk away. Behind them lights and shadows flickered on the walls. A television, probably. He watched for several minutes while shadows came in and out of view. There was no way to tell if anyone was being held captive without going inside, which would be impossible if the two thugs were home. He would have to come back later, maybe think of some way to get them out of the A-frame for an hour or so.

He waited for them to disappear from the window and then crept back up the trail into the forest. Once on the trail he backtracked to the Cherokee, making sure to dodge the dead coon. Then he drove back to Taos, continuing on past the Plaza on Paseo del Pueblo Sud to Lovato

Place, home of the Taos County Sheriff. The square concrete building was as ugly as sin and surrounded by a huge parking lot. Looked like old Hank had lots of business to keep him occupied. At the moment Kate Isaac's disappearance was considered a minor affair. That would change as soon as they learned it had turned in to kidnapping or, God forbid, murder. He parked the Cherokee and walked through the front door.

"Can I help you?" a woman behind the counter asked, a plump middle-aged woman with a friendly smile.

"Yeah, I'm here to see Hank." As he spoke he saw Hank in back berating one of his officers, hands waving in the air. He'd never seen Hank angry, but it looked like Hank could turn up the temperature when needed.

The junior officer kept nodding and then backed away slowly, away from Hank.

The woman behind the counter waved at Hank and said, "He's all yours. Good luck!"

Hank smiled when he saw Fernando approaching. "Howdy, Fernando. Did you find yer missin' woman?"

"No, it turns out she's been kidnapped," Fernando said.

'No shit? Just what I don't need to hear today. Well, hell, come on back."

Fernando followed Hank back to an office and took a chair across from the desk. While he watched, Hank removed his Stetson and carefully hung it on a rack behind the desk.

"I'm listening."

"So Rachel got the call yesterday," Fernando said. "The kidnappers want two hundred fifty thousand dollars delivered in cash come Noon tomorrow at the ski basin. The voice on the phone sounded to me like Tom Jensen, the groundskeeper at the Luhan House. So I tailed him to the Red Dog Brewery and saw him meeting with the two yokels in the Crown Vic who ran me off the road. I think the three of them might be working together. So today, when I paid a visit to Tom's trailer in Arroyo Seco, I spotted the Crown Vic and followed it to an old decrepit A-frame up in the foothills above Arroyo Seco. Bizarre place with signs and paintings all around, dead animals hanging from trees, crazy shit. I'm thinking Kate Isaacs might be held captive there, maybe in the barn out back."

Nodding, Hank said, "Yeah, now I remember that Crown Vic. It belongs to the McCullers brothers, Travis and Johnny. We had a problem with them a couple of years ago. They shot at a country tax assessor who came out to assess their property. Threatened him and raised all kinds of hell. It was a damn stupid thing to do because the assessor ended up lowering their taxes since the place has gone to hell in a hand-basket. Judge had to dismiss the case when the assessor didn't show up in court because he was scared of the McCullers. Can't blame him, they're a couple of crazy bastards, especially the older brother, Travis. The little one just goes along with Travis. I think he's a little slow."

"I can believe that, just looking at their yard."

"Hah! You oughta seen it when Trump ran for president the second time. They had flags and billboards plastered all over the roadside. I ain't no damn liberal, but I got nothing but contempt for that rich boy Trump and all his insults. Man needs to learn some manners."

"So are the brothers violent?"

"Can be, but their mama Lizzie usually keeps them outta trouble. Both of them are mama's boys. They take their walking orders from their mama. She's one strong woman."

"Would she tolerate kidnapping?"

Hank shook his head. "No, I can't imagine that. Lizzie keeps a tight rein on them boys. But listen, if you do go out there again, you best give me a call. They can get nasty."

Fernando nodded.

"In the mean-time we'll get Tom Jensen in for fingerprinting and a DNA test. Maybe he's our number six at the party Saturday. I never liked his looks much...that damned pony tail."

14

Fernando ate a quick lunch at a taco stand on the Plaza and then returned to the El Pueblo for a nap. He did some of his best thinking while napping. Somehow engaging the subconscious kick-started his thought process, revealing possibilities that his conscious self would never have recognized. He needed that extra firepower today, trying to figure out how to proceed with the kidnapping and the McCullers brothers. He was sound asleep on the bed when his damn cell phone buzzed and then rang on the bedside table.

He heard a woman's voice when he answered the phone.

"Detective Lopez, this is Francis from the Luhan House. You wanted me to call if there were developments...and you asked about Tom Jensen, if he had ever been in trouble with the law?"

"Yes, what's happened?" Fernando mumbled.

"He's being accused of killing Caitlin Adams, the woman who was murdered last Saturday. Some guy, apparently Caitlin's boyfriend, confronted him here and they got in a terrible fight."

"Are they still there?"

"Yes, and the sheriff just arrived," Francis said.

"Okay, I'll be right over."

Fernando grabbed what he needed in the room and then drove over to Morada Road. He spotted two sheriff's cars in the parking lot of the Luhan House. The action, though, was further up on the courtyard. Hank and his deputy had separated the two combatants, with Hank taking charge of Tom and one of his deputies manhandling an irate Billy Jackson. The deputy struggled to contain Billy, who continued to curse and yell insults. On the other hand Tom slumped forward on a bench near the front door, holding his head in his hands.

Coming closer, Fernando saw Tom's bloody face and smashed nose. Looked broken.

"Looks like we found our number six," Hank said as Fernando approached. "Turns out that Tom here drove Kate to Caitlin's house and then came back later to pick her up. Except Kate decided to walk back to the Luhan House all by her lonesome. At which point Tom and Caitlin got into a cat fight. They started arguing and pushing and shoving until Caitlin fell and hit her head on a coffee table. According to Tom, Caitlin pushed him first."

"What about Forensics?" Fernando asked.

"They identified Tom's DNA this morning."

Tom started wailing, head tucked low between his knees. "I fucked up! I didn't mean to hurt her. She was so drunk she could hardly stand up. She insulted me, saying I was white trash and Kate wanted nothing to do with a piece of shit like me. Then she shoved me and I shoved her back, that's all I did. I swear to God! I only touched her once, but she lost her balance and fell...."

"He killed her!" Billy screamed from across the courtyard. "What more do you need? Arrest the motherfucker!"

Hank shrugged. "Fernando? You got any questions for Mr. Jensen here before we take him in for a statement?"

"What about the kidnapping—how did you get involved in that?" Fernando asked Tom.

Tom moaned, watching blood drip from his nose onto his jeans. Drip, drip. Like sand in an hourglass.

"Answer the man!" Hank roared and kicked Tom hard in the shin.

"Owww!" Tom wailed. "Leave me alone. I want a lawyer!"

Hank sighed and waved over his deputy.

"Mike, take this sorry sonofabitch in for questioning, read him his rights, and let him call Legal Aid. I need to have a word with Mr. Jackson over there."

Mike grabbed Tom by the ponytail and pulled him off the bench. "Let's go!"

"Owww!" Tom continued to wail as Mike led him away by the ponytail.

Fernando watched the two of them walk down to the parking lot while Hank hitched up his trousers and headed for Billy. One look at Hank and Billy stopped his cursing. The big man with the wide-brimmed Stetson had that effect on people.

"Now! I'm not saying you didn't have cause to beat the shit out of that poor sucker, but what exactly did he tell you about what happened with Caitlin? And make it short, I ain't got all fuckin' day to waste on you punks."

Billy's eyes flashed and jumped in his skull. "He told me the same thing he told you! Except it's all bullshit! When I left her house Caitlin was too high to get into a shoving match with anyone. She might have mouthed off, because no one there liked Jensen. He's a loser. But she wouldn't have started a shoving match. That's not something Caitlin could have done in her condition. He's lying!"

Hank sighed. "So you said. Why didn't anyone like Jensen?"

"Because he's an asshole. And he's violent. His last girlfriend had to get a restraining order on him. You should know that, you're the fucking sheriff, right?"

Hank stared at Billy. "Watch your mouth, kid."

"It's the truth!"

Hank frowned. "I'll check it out. Tell me, are you still working at the rafting company in case I need to get in touch with you?"

Billy nodded.

"Alright, get the hell out of here before I change my mind. I just might bring you in for assault and battery. You understand?"

Billy nodded and moved away, walking slowly, tentatively.

Hank turned to Fernando. "This whole damn situation is starting to piss me off. And if Jensen is involved in this kidnapping with the McCullers it's only going to get worse."

"So what aren't you telling me about the McCullers?"

"Only that they're a bunch of backwoods, inbred crazies, that's what," Hank said, shaking his head. "I don't think the brothers even graduated from high school. The father was a no-account drunk, spent as much time in the drunk tank as he did at home. Used to beat Lizzie and the boys something fierce. Put Lizzie in the hospital a couple of times, broke her arm once. We tried to get her to leave the sonofabitch, but she refused. He disappeared about ten years ago, just up and abandoned the family. Hasn't been seen since. Lizzie raised them boys herself, kept 'em out of trouble all these years."

"Until now, that is."

"Maybe. What I'm trying to tell you is that these boys were abused. They were raised to be meaner than a rattlesnake. Over the years we've hauled them in more times than I can count."

"For what?" Fernando asked.

"You name it: fighting, shop-lifting, drag-racing, traffic violations, cruelty to animals, and shooting at a tax assessor who showed up at their property, which I already told you about. They get their kicks by torturing animals. Couple of years ago they had this sick game they thought was funny. They would trap animals in the national forest—which was legal in New Mexico until last year, you know—and they would hang the dead animals from trees or bushes along the hiking trails. Everything from coons to coyotes, even bobcats. Then they would hide off to the side of the trail and watch the hikers freak out. Real funny, huh?"

"Yeah, I saw one of those this morning on a trail behind their A-frame," Fernando said. "A coon."

"Shit! That means they're still doing it." Hank put his hands on his hips and surveyed the grounds. "So what's your plan? Noon tomorrow doesn't give you much time."

Fernando checked his watch. "Do you have time for a beer? The Taos Inn is just around the corner."

Hank smiled. "Does a bear shit in the woods?"

15

Saturday morning broke cool and breezy with thick gray clouds hovering over the mountains. Fernando woke up on edge, uncertain about what the day would bring. He was especially concerned that he hadn't been able to reach Rachel. He'd called several times last night but none of his calls had been answered. After leaving two messages on her machine, he gave up and decided to wait until this morning before trying again. She was scheduled to meet the kidnappers at Noon today up at the ski basin behind the Blake Hotel.

He waited until he finished his first cup of coffee and then dialed her number. He let it ring five, six times and was about to click off when she finally answered. "Mr. Lopez...I expected your call."

"Yeah, I called several times last night. Why didn't you pick up? We need to agree on a plan for meeting the kidnapers today."

"Actually, I'm not coming up to Taos."

"What? What did you say?"

"I'm not meeting the kidnappers. Kate visited me last night and told me not to worry, that she was okay. She said at first she was frightened but now everything is fine. She told me I should move on with my life."

Fernando almost dropped his cell phone. "Visited you? "What are you talking about?"

"She appeared to me. Like a vision. We're at peace now, both of us."

"Peace? She could be injured or dying. I think I know where they're hiding her, but we have to get her out fast before they kill her. Don't you understand?"

Silence.

"She's your partner! Don't you want her back?"

"I didn't get the money."

"Doesn't matter, I have a plan," Fernando said.

More silence.

"Rachel, listen! I want you to meet the kidnappers as planned. Noon, behind the Blake Hotel. Tell them you need a couple more days to get the money. They won't like it, but they'll agree because they have no other choice. I'll need at least half an hour to get Kate out of their compound. Can you do that? For Kate?"

He heard her breathing at the other end of the line.

"Okay...I suppose I can."

"Not good enough," Fernando said. "I need to be able to count on you. Will you be there?"

"Okay, yes," Rachel said finally.

So he explained his plan and told her about the McCullers, all the juicy details. "I need at least half an hour."

He began to worry as soon as their conversation ended. What if Rachel didn't show up at the ski basin? What if she couldn't delay the McCullers brothers? And what the hell was this craziness about Kate visiting her last night and telling her not to worry? Visions, apparitions, ghosts, he didn't like to acknowledge their existence, not even to himself. Like everyone else he pretended he lived in a rational universe. You had to pretend in order to function.

Feeling tense, he went to Michael's Kitchen for breakfast and then walked around the Plaza trying to relax. By the time he made it back to his room it was past 10 a.m. He sat in the easy chair by the window worrying about everything that could go wrong with his plan. His feeling was that everything that could go wrong, would go wrong. He was usually right. That meant when the time came he would have to adjust and readjust accordingly.

He considered coordinating with Hank, or at least asking Hank for backup, but the logistics presented too many problems. Better if it remained a two-person operation. If Rachel didn't show, then he would be in big trouble.

At 10:30 he grabbed his holster and binoculars and walked out to the Cherokee. He drove slowly, no need to hurry, arriving at the forest road above the McCullers A-frame thirty minutes later. The foothills were socked in with low-hanging clouds, the tops of the tall ponderosa pines lost in a thick fog. He parked in the trees and put on his holster. The binoculars he decided to leave behind. Less weight to carry. As before he followed the trail past where the dead coon hung from a tree and around to the half-buried boulder. He ducked behind the boulder, watching the A-frame and the Ford Vic parked out front.

He breathed a great sigh of relief when he spotted Rachel's Beamer driving by on the road. She hadn't let him down. His plan just might work.

Several minutes later the two McCullers brothers walked out of the house, the tall thin brother leading the way and the short roly-poly one following behind. Both men wore brown Carhartt jackets and jeans. The older brother wore a concealed carry holster. The younger one carried what looked like a shotgun, probably a twelve-gauge. Kate was not with them. The brothers climbed into the Crown Vic and drove off fast up the road toward the ski basin.

He waited a few minutes to make sure they didn't suddenly return for whatever reason. He saw no sign of Lizzie, the mother, or any activity in the house. So he crept out from behind the boulder and moved slowly down the hill. Toward the bottom he noticed what looked like an old-fashioned root cellar dug out of the hillside, with a stone front and a rusted metal door. A large padlock, also rusted, secured the door of the cellar. At first he wondered if he'd found where the McCullers were holding Kate captive. Seemed too easy. Then he noticed the cobwebs hanging from the doorframe. Clearly no one had opened the door recently.

He looked around to make sure no one was watching from the A-frame. Then he took out his lock pick and went to work on the padlock. The lock was frozen from non-use. He couldn't get the locking mechanism to release the shackle. Without lubricant, the only thing he could think to do was spit into the keyhole and move the pick from side to side. He kept trying until the mechanism started to move. With one last pull he sprang the lock.

He removed the padlock from the door, careful not to make any noise. He placed the padlock in the weeds along the stone wall and tried the door. The door wouldn't budge. Using the full weight of his body, he pushed against the door with his shoulder.

When this didn't work, he grabbed the door handle with both hands and shook it up and down. Then he stood back, leaned against the door, and pushed with both hands. The door opened a couple of inches, scraping against the jam. He kept pushing in quick spurts until he had the door opened a good eighteen inches, wide enough for him to slide through.

A dank musty smell flooded his senses as he edged through the door. He gave his eyes time to adjust to the dark interior and then stepped forward into the darkness. Except the floor wasn't where it should have been. He pitched forward, tumbling down an earthen stairway dug out of the hill and falling into what turned out to be a pile of bones. He rose up on his hands and knees, hearing some of the small bones snap under his weight. When his eyes adjusted to the dim light he saw bones littering the entire floor of the dug out. Looked like bones from dogs or other large animals, complete with skulls. Most of the leg and rib bones were large. Big dogs. Or maybe coyotes or bobcats.

Steadying himself, he managed to stand up and maintain his balance. He saw something ahead in the darkness. A beam of light from outside illuminated something glowing on what looked like a table. He took a small, cautious step forward, wary of what he could not see. Then another. Suddenly he saw and jumped back in surprise. It was a body, a badly decomposed body, lying spread-eagle on a sheet of plywood. The plywood rested on cement blocks stacked waist high.

He moved forward to get a better look, remembering that his cell phone had a flashlight function. He took it out of his pocket and shined a feeble light on what was left of the body. The hands and feet had rotted to bare bones. Loose strands of fraying rope wrapped around the exposed bones, suggesting the body had been tied down on the table while dead or maybe alive crucifixion style. The rest of the sunken body was clothed in faded garments and resembled a bag of bones.

He inched closer, noticing patches of blackened skin and tufts of hair clinging to the bare skull. In the dim light its hollow eye sockets became black holes. When he saw a third hole in the center of the forehead he became suspicious. He leaned over the body to examine what looked like a bullet entry wound. As he suspected the back of the skull had been blown away and a bullet lodged in the plywood. The deceased had been tied down and executed on the table.

The identity of the deceased came as no surprise. He knew as soon as he spotted another sheet of plywood behind the makeshift table. This one was vertical and stood behind the funeral bier. Someone had spray painted the words "Pops R I Hell" in red paint on the plywood. That served as a headstone for the McCullers father who had been missing for ten years.

Clearly Pops had been dead for most of those ten years. But time was short. He needed to find Kate before the McCullers brothers returned. So he climbed the earthen steps and eased out of the door, leaving it ajar to save time.

Now he had to worry about the mother, Lizzie. Would she be in the house waiting for him with a shotgun in her lap? Maybe she'd seen him open the door to the dug out. Maybe she was overprotective of her two sons.

He crossed the back yard, weaving through the abandoned vehicles and rusted appliances and mounds of trash. He found the back screen door hanging open, so he stepped inside without bothering to knock. The kitchen looked lived in, with a few dishes on the counters, but nothing like the mess he'd found in Tom Jensen's trailer. But as he walked through the other rooms he saw the dysfunction. All the rooms were coated with dust. Dirt and even chunks of dried mud littered the floors.

The dining room table and chairs had been pushed to one side of the room to make room for a dozen or so animal traps. He saw everything from light-weight Tomahawk cage traps to heavy-duty Duke jaws traps for large animals. All lined up against the wall, ready for action.

Next door the former living room looked more like a camping store, with camping and fishing equipment piled everywhere. Coleman tents and propane camping stoves, sleeping bags and coolers and lanterns stacked along one wall. Surrounded by fishing poles and tackle, two recliners faced a portable television placed on the fireplace mantle. Looked like a bachelor pad to him. Hard to imagine any mother would tolerate a mess like this.

Down the hall to the front door he saw holes punched or kicked out of the drywall. Beside the door stood a loaded twelve-gauge shotgun ready for action. He pitied the poor stranger who wandered up to this door. He started up a narrow staircase to the second floor, the floorboards creaking. At the top of the stairs he found an open closet containing a small armory of weapons: shotguns, rifles, and semi-automatic pistols. Not a good sign.

He moved on down the upper hallway checking the bedrooms as he went. The first two were as cluttered as the rooms downstairs, with outdoor clothing and stacks of ammo piled on the floor. Both had unmade single beds with sleeping bags instead of blankets. Walking down the hall to the room at the end he smelled a familiar fragrance: piñon wood. The smell grew stronger as he approached the door, which was locked. He knocked on the door and waited for a response. None came. So he took out his lock pick once again and went to work on the lock. Moments later the lock clicked open.

As soon as he opened the door his senses were assaulted by the strong, biting odor of piñon incense laced with an undercurrent of something else, a putrid smell. He stepped through the door into a semi-dark room. Heavy curtains and shades smothered the windows. A small candle burned on a makeshift altar on the far wall, alongside sticks of burning incense that sent streamers of smoke swirling in the feeble light of the candle. Next to the altar he saw a woman sitting up in bed staring at him.

He jumped. "Mrs. McCullers?"

16

"Mrs. McCullers?" Fernando asked again.

No response.

He took one step forward, then another. The plank floor squeaked and moaned as he approached the bed. It took him a moment to realize the woman was dead, had been dead for some time. Standing this close the sharp smell of piñon and decomposing flesh nearly gagged him. She sat upright under a blanket with her hands folded in her lap. In the candlelight her shriveled face was splotched yellow and ashen black under a shroud of gray hair. Her half-open eyes gazed straight ahead at nothing. The skin around her open mouth had shrunk back, exposing her teeth and gums. As though she had been trying to say something when the moment of death arrived.

While he stared at the dead woman he began to hear voices, whispers coming from somewhere. Barely audible, they made a buzzing sound. Or maybe it was only the wind.

Finally the ghastly sight made him turn away, but as he did her hand seemed to rise up from the blanket. When he looked again the hand was resting in her lap. Had he imagined the hand rising? He moved toward the altar beside the bed. Lined up along the wall were photos of the woman when younger. A rosary lay on top of an ancient Bible, its leather binding in tatters. While he looked around he heard the whispering sound again. Was the sound coming from the corpse? He didn't wait to find out, hurrying out of the room and closing the door softly behind him.

He stood in the empty hallway a moment to gather his wits, trying to put the dead woman out of his mind. Then he checked his watch. Already fifteen minutes past Noon and he had not yet found Kate Isaacs.

He hurried down the stairs and out the back door, heading for the shed on the far side of the house. The shed was his last best hope, a rough wooden structure with a flat tin roof. He found another padlock on the door, but this one looked brand new and he was able to open it quickly with his pick. Then he stepped into what looked like a two-room workshop. A workbench and wooden chair occupied most of the front room, with tools on the bench and hanging from the walls. Tools for everyday use and some specialized woodworking tools: awls, chisels, clamps, and various saws. Nothing out of the ordinary for a tool shed.

He walked around a half wall to the back room, which turned out to be a storage area. Lots of stacked boxes along with shovels, axes, chain saws and other land maintenance implements. Then he spotted it and his spirits sank. Along the side wall, pushed in a corner, stood a large white freezer. Horizontal, about seven feet wide and four feet tall, more than large enough to hold a human body, especially a small woman. He hesitated, not sure what to do. Did he want to open the freezer or leave it to Hank? He knew instinctively what he would find. Call it an intuition, a morbid expectation based on what he had just seen in the house and the hillside mausoleum. He'd walked into a fucking necropolis.

In the end he couldn't just walk away. He had to see for himself. So he went to the freezer and opened the lid. There she was. On top of packages wrapped in white butcher paper lay the frosted corpse of a small woman wearing a nightgown. Frozen, with frost covering her arms and the other exposed parts of her body. A black cloth bag covered her head. Drawstrings on the bag had been pulled tight around her neck, leaving a visible indentation mark. She looked like a manikin bent at the waist and stuffed in a freezer.

He closed the lid, having seen enough. Time to contact Hank. He rushed to the door and pushed it open. Too late. He heard the roar of the Crown Vic turning into the driveway. Now what?

Fernando closed the door. Then he worried the McCullers would notice the padlock on the outside of the door was unlocked. He watched through the side window as the Crown Vic pulled up beside the A-frame. He was surprised to see three people in the car, not two. The two brothers jumped out first. He got a good look at them this time. Travis, the older brother, stood a good six inches taller than Johnny, his younger brother. Travis had a scruffy gray beard and a weathered face, while Johnny was round with a baby face.

Travis walked around the Crown Vic to the passenger's side and opened the rear door. He reached in and grabbed the occupant and pulled her out of the car. It was Rachel, wearing slacks and a tight leather jacket. She struggled with Travis, even though she was bound and gagged with her hands taped together behind her back. Travis cursed and shoved her toward the shed. She fell in the dirt and tried to crawl away on her knees, but Travis kicked her in the back and sent her sprawling toward the shed. Then he picked her up by the hair and escorted her the rest of the way.

Fernando ducked to the side of the window and looked for a hiding place. He found one in the back room, behind a stack of boxes. It would have to do. The only other option was to crawl into the freezer with Kate. If he did that, how the hell would he ever get out?

Fernando heard the door open.

"Get in," Travis said, still struggling with Rachel. They shuffled inside. "Sit her down on the chair and tape her legs to the chair."

Rachel mumbled something as she plopped down in the chair beside the workbench.

"Now take her gag off."

Rachel sputtered and started to cough. It took her several seconds to get her breath.

"Okay, last chance," Travis said, growing impatient. "Where's the money?"

'Yeah...or we'll fuck you up," said Johnny, the younger brother.

"I told you...it's hidden until you show me Kate."

"No!" Travis roared. "Here's what's gonna happen. I'll give you one more chance, and then I'm gonna turn you over to Johnny here. Johnny loves to cause pain. His favorite hobby is torturing animals. He's gonna start by pulling out your fingernails, one at a time. Then he's gonna start pulling out your teeth with pliers. When you pass out, as you will, he'll just wake you up with cold water and continue where he left off. Have you ever had a tooth pulled without anesthetic?"

Rachel sobbed. "Please, don't hurt me. I beg you!"

"Then tell us where you hid the money."

"Okay," she sputtered. "It's in front of the Blake. In a small suitcase under a tarp covering one of the big heaters."

"One suitcase?"

"Just one. I could only get fifties."

"Shall I get the pliers?" Johnny asked.

"I'm telling the truth," Rachel pleaded.

Silence.

Then Travis spoke: "Let's hope you're telling the truth, lady. We'll leave you here while Johnny and I go get the suitcase. If it's not there... well, you already know what he'll do."

"I'll fuck you up," the younger brother repeated.

"Save it! Now put the gag back on and let's go." Travis barked.

Rachel struggled in the chair, gagging.

The door closed and the lock clicked.

Fernando waited behind the boxes until he heard the Crown Vic drive off.

When he stepped into the front room Rachel jumped up and down on the chair. "MMMM!...MMMM!"

Fernando checked the window to make sure the car was gone. Then he took out his pocketknife and cut the tape on her hands and ankles. Finally he removed her gag.

She shook her head. "Fucking pigs! Fucking men! You're all alike!"

He glanced at her. "You might be right, but we need to get out of here."

"I can't leave without Kate."

"I don't think she's alive, Rachel." He decided not to tell her about the freezer. Not now. They had to leave before the McCullers returned.

"What do you mean?"

"Just that. Did you really bring the money after all?"

She shook her head. "No, I just told them that to buy some time. Figured I'd find a way to get out."

"What if you didn't?"

She shrugged.

"You're a brave woman, but these guys are dangerous. Let's go!"

He picked up the chair and carried it into the storage room. "Stand back.

While she waited in the doorway, he picked up the chair and smashed it through the rear window. He used a crowbar he'd found on the tool bench to bust out the glass fragments sticking to the frame. Then he pushed the chair under the window and said, "You go first."

He helped her up on the chair and through the window and then followed. The two of them sprinted toward the boulder and the forest trail that would take them to safety.

17

"Where are we going?" Rachel asked, following Fernando on the trail.

'To my car. It's not far."

They rounded the curve and climbed the rise where the raccoon still hung from a tree. She stopped to take a look at the coon. "Christ! What's this supposed to be? A warning or something?"

"Well, it's not an invitation...."

She gave him a dirty look.

Just then they heard the Crown Vic come roaring down the highway back to the A-frame. It wouldn't take them long to discover Rachel was gone. That meant their window of opportunity was short.

He jogged over the last leg of the trail, with Rachel running close behind. When he reached the Cherokee he jumped in and waited for Rachel. As she closed her door he fired the engine and backed up quickly. Then he shot out from behind the trees, turning sharply onto the two-lane. He turned right toward Arroyo Seco and Taos and gunned the engine.

"Wait, I need to get my car," she said.

"Later. Right now we need to get out of here fast and find help."

He pushed the Cherokee beyond the speed he would normally drive on a mountain road until they drove by the A-frame. Then he slowed down, thinking they would have clear sailing the rest of the way. Big mistake, he soon discovered.

Coming around a tight turn he saw the Crown Vic up ahead. The big Ford slowed to a stop and then turned sideways blocking the road.

"What the fuck?" he said out loud.

Then his instincts took over. He twisted the steering wheel to the left, spinning around and swerving into the ditch. The big wheels of the Cherokee spun wildly, kicking up dust and rocks.

In the rear view mirror he saw the McCullers climbing out of the

Grand Vic. The older brother had a rifle in his hand.

He stomped on the accelerator. The Cherokee fish-tailed until the wheels caught and they sped up the road. Their only play now was to make it to the Ski Basin and call for help. Call Hank.

Rachel held on to the door handle as he turned one sharp corner after another. It seemed to take forever, but they reached Ski Village with no sign of the McCullers behind them.

Rachel pointed to a parking lot near the Blake Hotel. "Stop there at my car I need to get something."

He slammed on the brakes and turned into the parking lot. He saw no one around who could help them. The place looked deserted now that skiing season was over.

"Oh shit!" Rachel said when she saw her BMW. The windshield had been smashed and the tires punctured. Flat as a pancake.

She jumped out and ran over to her car, opened the driver's door and grabbed a small pistol. Looked like a small Glock, maybe a G43. A moment later she climbed back in the Cherokee.

She looked at him. "I'll shoot the bastard if he tries to touch me again."

He nodded, not about to say anything, and then hit the gas. He drove around the loop and parked behind the Ski Valley offices, where the Cherokee couldn't be seen from the highway. That would buy them some time.

They bailed out of the Cherokee and ran toward the nearest ski run, the Edelweiss.

"Where are you going?" she asked.

"Better to be up high. We can hide in the trees."

They started the long climb up the slope staying just inside the pines. Before long he started huffing and puffing. It had been a long time since he'd hiked in the mountains. Not long enough.

She passed him halfway up the first hill. "You okay?"

He ignored her.

They stopped on top of the second hill. From their position in the trees they watched the Crown Vic arrive at the ski basin. The big Ford slowed to a stop and then began to drive up and down the roads crisscrossing the village. Finally it stopped in the parking lot near the Blake Hotel, next to Rachel's car.

The McCullers climbed out of the Crown Vic and stood there scanning the dozen or so ski runs on the mountain. Next the two brothers walked over to the ski lift and around behind the Blake. Finally they gave up and returned to the Crown Vic. Then they started arguing. Suddenly

Travis shouted something and pushed Johnny into the side of the Ford. Johnny fought back and tried to tackle Travis, who pushed him to the ground and kicked him in the stomach. Johnny screamed and lay still while Travis stood over him yelling. This went on for several minutes. Finally they climbed back in the Crown Vic and drove off.

"Looks like we dodged a bullet," Fernando said, watching the Crown Vic drive off down the highway.

"Now what?"

"I need to call the sheriff. You better call a tow truck and have your car towed into town. Have them take it to an auto shop that can replace the windshield and also fix the tires."

So while she searched online for a towing service in Taos he wandered on down the slope. When he reached the bottom he took out his cell phone and called Hank. He wanted to avoid talking in the presence of Rachel, who didn't yet know about Kate.

Hank answered immediately. "Howdy, Fernando. What's up?"

"I found Kate. She's dead."

"Well, shit! Where'd you find her?"

"Out at the McCullers place," Fernando said. "Stuffed in a freezer inside their shed. Looks like she was strangled. There's a cloth bag over her head with the drawstrings pulled tight."

"How in hell did you get access to that?" Hank asked.

"I had Rachel meet the kidnappers at the money drop to give me time to search the premises. Good thing I did, because I found two other bodies out there—the McCullers mother and father."

"What? Lizzie?"

"Both of them," Fernando said. "The father's in a kind of mausoleum dug out of the hill behind the house and the mother's in a bedroom upstairs. It's not a pretty sight, Hank."

"That explains why I haven't seen her around lately. Okay. So where are you now?"

"I'm up at the ski basin, where the money exchange was supposed to occur."

Fernando explained what happened when the McCullers discovered Rachel hadn't brought the money, and how he and Rachel managed to escape and hide out at the ski basin.

"So is Rachel with you now?"

"Yeah, she's probably going to have to spend the night in Taos. The brothers did a number on her car. She's having it towed now."

"Fucking McCullers!" Hank said. "I've known them boys since they were pups. Mean little shits, both of them."

"We're going to need your help, Hank."

"No problem. I can meet you at the A-frame in an hour. Can you be there?"

"I'll be there. Oh...and one more thing. I haven't yet told Rachel that Kate's dead."

Hank whistled. "Why not?"

"I just haven't had the heart. I know I have to tell her. Just have to find the right time."

Hank laughed. "Well you better do it soon. With three bodies on the premises, I'm gonna have to call forensics. You don't want Rachel to be there when they pull Kate out of the freezer. At least give her some warning."

"Yeah...I know. I'll do it," he said, watching Kate talking on her cell phone.

"Okay, Fernando. See you in twenty."

Fernando put his phone away and headed back up the slope to face the music.

18

Rachel broke down when Fernando told her Kate was dead. He didn't mention finding her body in the freezer. Just didn't seem necessary to share the sordid details. She would find out in due time, he supposed. She hugged him and then sobbed quietly on his shoulder for several minutes. Finally she pulled away and dried her eyes and then sat down on a bed of pine needles under a massive Ponderosa. She closed her eyes, rocking back and forth.

"I guess I knew she was gone...just didn't want to admit it," she said. "I blame myself. I should have come up with the money right away. She would still be alive if I had."

"No, you can't blame yourself," Fernando said. "We know who's responsible. They'll be held accountable."

She took a tissue out of a pocket and wiped her eyes again. "God, I hate that house, the Luhan House! I told her not to go. Lots of bad things happened there. Too many ghosts."

"Yeah?"

She managed a forced laugh. "We argued about it all the time. Her work. She was always going to these old places to dig up stories about famous women who lived a long time ago. Stirring up the past...stirring up the ghosts. Bringing back all the bad memories. Why couldn't she leave the dead alone? I told her over and over: let them go, they're dead. Don't bring back their ghosts to haunt you. Because that's what they did, they haunted her night and day. She couldn't escape them. It got so bad that she could hardly sleep at night. I couldn't take it. I told her if she didn't stop obsessing over these dead people I would have to move out. That's how serious it was."

Fernando didn't know what to say. So he said nothing.

By the time the tow truck arrived from Taos he was already late for meeting Hank at the A-frame. They walked down the slope to meet the driver, a big man in overalls and a backwards baseball cap. He had tattoos on both arms and a smile on his face. "That's a hell of a way to treat a Beamer."

"Can you repair it?" Rachel asked.

The big man nodded. "Yeah, we'll fix the tires and get B and M Glass to drop in a new windshield. Should be ready tomorrow morning sometime."

"So I'll have to spend the night," she said to Fernando.

"No problem," Fernando responded. "Have him drop you off at the El Pueblo Lodge next to Michael's. Ask for the room next to mine. That way I can keep you safe. I'll be there as soon as I can."

"The El Pueblo...?"

"Yeah, the motor lodge across the street from the Kachina. Not great, but one night's not so bad."

She nodded, sort of, and turned away.

Fernando watched Rachel climb into the front of the truck alongside the driver and take off, with the BMW loaded on the flat bed of the truck.

Already a half hour late, he returned to his Cherokee and breathed a sigh of relief when he saw the McCullers hadn't touched it. He drove back down the highway. He slowed down approaching the A-frame, wanting to make sure the brothers were nowhere in sight. He saw Hank's cruiser when he turned into the driveway, but not Hank. He parked behind the cruiser and started walking toward the shed when he saw Hank step out the back door of the A-frame. Hank was shaking his head and talking to himself.

Hank removed his Stetson and scratched his head. He nodded to Fernando. "Well, I for damn sure never seen anything like that before."

"Not outside a mortuary, anyway," Fernando said.

"Not even there. Ole Lizzie sittin' up in bed like that, half decomposed. Not embalmed. It's disrespectful, that's what I think."

Fernando looked around. "No sign of the brothers."

"None. Forensics should be here soon. They'll examine the body and make a determination about what to do next. I put a handkerchief over my nose and pulled down the blanket but didn't see any indication of foul play. Looks like a natural death to me. If they agree, they'll call the state department of health and report the body. Someone will have to get a death certificate and bury her. And fast, because the decomposing body is a health risk. Plus it stinks like a sonofabitch!"

"So you saw the father?"

"Pops? Yeah, the crypt was my first stop. That's bad enough, with the goddamn skull sticking out of the shirt. Pieces of black skin still hanging from his jowls. God almighty!" Hank shook his head sadly and kicked at the dirt. "So what about Kate? Where's this freezer you mentioned?"

"This way," Fernando said, heading for the shed. Hank followed. The door was still open, so they stepped inside. "The freezer's in the back storage area."

Hank led the way to the freezer. Fernando stayed back, not wanting to view Kate's remains for a second time. Once was enough.

Hank threw open the freezer and stood back. He said nothing for a moment. Then he turned to Fernando. "So where's the body?"

"What do you mean?" Fernando stepped forward and looked into the freezer. He saw nothing but packages of venison wrapped in white butcher paper. "I don't understand. The body's gone."

Hank gave him a stern look. "You haven't been seeing things lately, have you old buddy?"

He laughed. "Hah! I swear to God the body was here this morning."

"Well, hell...that means the boys came back to get her. To hide the body somewhere else."

They walked back outside into bright sunshine refracted through the pines. Hank walked to his cruiser and leaned back on its fender. Fernando followed.

"If they wanted, they could dump the body anywhere," Hank said. "On the other hand, if they felt they could ransom the body, they would hide it. Somewhere like Tom Jensen's trailer, for example. If Tom didn't have legal problems of his own, that might be the place to start looking for the body. But Tom's in jail at the moment, or was when I left the office, so I think the brothers will stay clear of the trailer."

Fernando nodded. "Will they release Jensen?"

"Probably, unless they can find some hard evidence," Hank said. "But I don't think the McCullers will go anywhere near that trailer. Not with Jensen's trouble with the law."

Hank stood up straight and looked around. "This place is downright depressing. I swear I can still smell the stink from Lizzie's body."

"And Pops'," Fernando added.

"You know, there is one other place that comes to mind," Hank continued. "A cabin in the mountains here, about five miles away on an old abandoned forest road. Their daddy built the cabin twenty, thirty years ago. Ole McCullers was a trapper and a poacher. He slaughtered just about anything he could catch, legal or illegal, and sold the meat in town out of the back of his pickup. Did a fair business until one of the ranchers nearby caught him slaughtering one of his cows and beat hell out of him and then took him to court. McCullers ended up paying a fine instead of doing jail time, but after that he slaughtered mostly wild animals. Mostly.

"Anyway, McCullers built this cabin illegally on National Forest land and used it for his trapping. Very primitive, no running water, not even an outhouse. He was told to take it down but never did. I guess the rangers just left it up for hikers and cross-country skiers to use. To my knowledge no one's used it for years. I think it's still there."

"Okay, when do we leave?" Fernando asked.

"Whoa! Hold on to your horses, mister. It's a long hike—take us half a day at least. I'll need to get a deputy to go along with us, probably Dave. He's the best sharpshooter I have. We'll need backup because these McCullers boys are armed to the teeth and dangerous. They're survivalists. They know this forest like the back of their hand."

"Oh, I think we can handle the McCullers," Fernando said. "It's mostly the older brother, as far as I can tell."

"Yeah, Travis is the leader. Johnny just follows along."

Fernando waited while Hank made up his mind.

Hank checked his cell phone. "Suppose we meet you here tomorrow morning, say about ten."

"Sounds good. The sooner the better. I need to get back to Santa Fe."

"Meantime, I'll stick around for forensics. They best come soon—I'm sure as hell not sticking around after dark."

"What do you mean?" Fernando asked.

Hank rolled his eyes. "Did you take a good look at Lizzie up there? She has her slippers right there beside her bed and a half-drunk glass of water on the bedside table. What's that all about? Now I ain't exactly superstitious, but then again I don't want to press my luck. You understand?"

"I do."

"What we have here is a goddamned necropolis. You can count me out!"

19

On his way back to Taos Fernando decided to stop by Tom Jensen's trailer in Arroyo Hondo. Just to make sure the McCullers brothers hadn't been there and left a little something behind. When he turned off the highway he saw Tom's orange Wrangler and a Taos Police Department cruiser parked in front of the trailer. He pulled up beside the police cruiser as a uniformed officer stepped out of the trailer and said something to whoever was inside, presumably Tom.

Fernando walked up and introduced himself to the officer, a young cop with a crew cut and dark sunglasses. He explained he was working with Hank Mathews on the Kate Isaacs kidnapping."

The young cop smiled. "Well, if you're working with Hank Mathews you're in good hands. I just gave Jensen a ride home after he was released. The D.A. didn't have enough evidence to bring charges in the Adams homicide. All the investigation was able to establish was that she and Jensen argued, after which she fell and hit her head on a metal file cabinet. Her fall caused the fatal bleed. There were no other wounds on the body. Plus her blood alcohol was three times the legal limit, so there's not much of a case."

"What about the Isaacs kidnapping?"

"I hear he's cut a plea deal. He agreed to plead guilty to lesser accessory charges in turn for testifying against the McCullers brothers. Everyone's happy. I think."

"No kidding," Fernando said.

The young cop saluted and then climbed into his cruiser.

Fernando watched the cruiser drive off, its wheels kicking up dust all the way to the highway. Then he turned and walked up the steps and into the trailer.

The police had done a number when they searched the trailer, pouring out the contents of drawers and overturning everything that could be overturned. Tom sat on a dirty plaid sofa drinking a can of Coors. His face still looked like raw hamburger meat.

Tom frowned and raised his beer. "What is this? Open house week?"

Fernando ignored the question. "So you pled out in the kidnapping."

"That's what they tell me."

"How did you get involved in this anyway?" Fernando asked.

Tom sighed. "The McCullers had this kidnapping scheme for a long time. They were just waiting for someone worth kidnapping. They wanted me to find a celebrity, someone with money, staying at the Luhan House. I gave them Kate Isaacs name because I knew she was something of a celebrity, at least in Santa Fe. Anybody who can afford to live in Santa Fe these days is a rich motherfucker. Bunch of rich, privileged fucks!"

Tom spit on the floor of his trailer.

Fernando raised his hand. "Not everybody."

"The McCullers said they would split the ransom three ways if I would make the phone calls. I said yes, what the hell. They did the kidnapping and all the dirty work, not me."

"So how did Kate end up dead?"

"The cloth hood. They pulled the drawstrings too tight and cut off her air Dumb fuckers. They were never very bright. I've known them for years—since high school. A couple of losers. I should have known better than to get involved with them."

"But you were with them when they grabbed her," Fernando said. "Why didn't you try to stop them?"

Tom shook his head. "No, I drove over to Caitlin's to give Kate a ride back to the Luhan House, but she'd already gone. She decided to walk. So after I argued with Caitlin, I just went on home."

"Hah! You did more than argue. You got into a shoving match and she ended up dead."

"Yeah, but that was her fault. She was stumbling drunk, grabbing me all over and then shoving me. Finally she stumbled backwards and hit her head on the file cabinet. I just left. I got the hell out of there fast because I knew I would be blamed for what happened."

"You could have at least called nine-one-one," Fernando responded.

"Yeah, but like I said, I was afraid I'd be blamed."

Fernando stared at him, unable to decide if he was telling the truth.

"So tell me more about what happened when the McCullers grabbed Kate and put the hood on her head."

Tom chugged his Coors and tossed the empty can on the floor of the Airstream. "All I know is what they told me. They said they planned to break into her room and kidnap her there. But when they arrived at the Luhan House the door to her room was open and she was missing. They finally found her walking behind the house in her nightgown. That's where they grabbed her and pulled the hood over her head. What they told me anyway. Like I said, I wasn't there."

"What was she doing walking outside in her nightgown? "Fernando asked. "Did they have any idea?"

"Ghosts! The ghosts drove her out, like I told you earlier. All the bedrooms in the Luhan House are haunted, especially Mabel's bedroom. Last year the Taos paranormals recorded Dennis Hopper's voice up there, along with the voices of Mabel and some of her friends."

Fernando ignored the ghosts. "So, then, after they killed Kate the brothers took the body to their A-frame on the road to the ski basin?"

"I guess. I stay away from that fucking place."

"What, you don't like the vibes?" Fernando asked.

"The place creeps me out," Tom said. "It's like walking into some Edgar Allen Poe story. Last time I was there they showed me what they'd done with Pops—stuck him in a fucking dug-out behind their house to decompose. Stinks to high heaven. Have you seen it?"

Fernando nodded. "When did you see the brothers last?"

"Later that night. They stopped by my trailer to tell me Kate was dead. They had her stuffed in their trunk. Just what I wanted to hear. Now it was murder as well as kidnapping. I told them to get the hell off my land, that I hadn't agreed to be involved in murder."

"And yet you made the phone calls," Fernando said.

"Well...I'd already agreed to do that. I figured if there was a ransom, why shouldn't I get something in recompense...."

"Recompense?"

The word hung in the heavy air of the filthy trailer. They stared at each other, neither of them speaking.

Finally Fernando turned and walked out of the trailer into the fresh air. He stopped to admire the sunset, the western sky painted in pink and scarlet ribbons. After a moment he stepped down from the porch and went to his Cherokee. He took his time driving back to Taos. He'd been rushing around all day and just wanted to relax without worrying about the McCullers. Or about what tomorrow would bring when he and Hank went looking for them up on the mountain.

The El Pueblo lights shone bright as he pulled into the darkening parking lot. Inside he found a woman he'd not seen before, a redhead with shoulder-length hair and bright red lipstick. She smiled at him as he walked into the office.

"You must be Mr. Lopez," she said.

"That's me. I need to re-up for another night."

"Oh...I thought they put you on the weekly rate. I'm just here part-time," she explained, going to the desktop computer. "Yes, you're on the weekly rate. You're already covered."

"Thanks. Also, I need to find out what room Rachel Wolfe is in. She checked in this afternoon."

"Hmmm, I don't remember that name," she said. "I've been here all afternoon, but let me check."

Fernando waited while she went back to the computer and clicked through the files.

She glanced over at him. "No, I'm sorry, no one by that named checked in today."

He was stunned. "There must be some mistake. She was supposed to check in mid-afternoon, maybe two or three o'clock."

She shook her head. "I just don't see a registration under that name."

"Maybe she used a pseudonym. Small woman, mid forties, red hair with a streak of blue down her forehead. You wouldn't forget her."

"I'm sorry, but the only woman to check in so far today was an older woman with gray hair and glasses."

Fernando stood there for a moment before thanking the woman and stepping out of the office. He went directly to his room and called Rachel on his cell phone. She didn't answer, so he called again. No answer.

He sat down in the chair by the window and looked out on the dark, nearly empty parking lot. He didn't like this turn of events. Why wasn't Rachel answering her phone? She couldn't have gone back to Santa Fe without her car. Maybe the Beamer had been repaired this afternoon. That didn't seem very likely. Or maybe the McCullers had caught up with her before she reached the El Pueblo. He feared that scenario was the most likely.

He brooded over what to do until half past six. Then he walked over to Michael's Kitchen for a quick dinner. Back at the El Pueblo he called Estelle and told her he would have to spend another night in Taos. Then he kept trying Rachel every half hour. At eleven o'clock, exhausted, he threw himself on the bed and called it a day.

Now both Kate and Rachel were missing. Two lost ladies.

20

Hank and his deputy stood next to their cruiser talking when Fernando arrived at the A-frame Sunday morning. Hank waved as Fernando parked the Cherokee and walked over to meet them. The deputy ignored him, busy assembling what looked like a damned M4 assault rifle. Old Hank and his deputy meant business, clearly. Maybe he'd underestimated the McCullers brothers. To him they seemed a couple of sadistic louts with a sick interest in necrophilia.

"Fernando, this is Dave," Hank said. "Dave, Fernando."

They nodded at each other.

"Fernando, you can ride with us. I've got everything we'll need in the cruiser: water, medical supplies, and lots of ammunition."

"Are these guys really that dangerous?"

"We don't know," Hank said, "but we're for damned sure gonna be prepared if they are."

Fernando climbed into the rear seat of the cruiser and let Hank do the driving. Dave rode shotgun. Hank fired the engine and then drove down the highway a couple of hundred yards. Then he turned into what at first looked like a shallow arroyo with a sandy bottom. Quickly, though, the arroyo became a narrow forest service road littered with rocks and choked with weeds. Almost immediately the cruiser started bouncing up and down over the rough terrain.

Hank slowed to a crawl as weeds scraped the undercarriage of the cruiser. He had to stop altogether when they came upon a scattering of bushel-sized boulders in their path. It was either a rockslide from the hill above or a warning to go no further.

Fernando and Dave jumped out of the cruiser and rolled the boulders off to the side of the road while Hank waited impatiently behind the wheel.

Ever slower, they inched their way up the incline into the tall ponderosa pines. Eventually they approached a narrow clearing where they spotted something shiny ahead. Coming closer, they found the Crown Vic parked off to the side of the road behind Kate Isaac's blue Passat. Beyond the cars the road seemed to disappear, becoming no wider than an animal trail. Not only that, but someone had piled up deadwood and tree branches to block access to the trail. Hanging from a tree on the other side of the blockade was a piece of plywood. On the plywood someone had spray-painted a skull and bones with black paint. The paint had run, giving the impression of a skull melting off the wood.

"Yep, friendly people, the McCullers," Hank said, pulling up behind the Crown Vic.

Fernando laughed. "No shit! Tell me, have you been to this cabin? You know where it's located?"

Hank climbed out of the cruiser and stretched. "Only once, back when the Forest Service got after them to take down the cabin. Must be ten, twelve years ago. It's about a two-mile hike from here. You guys up for a little exercise?"

Dave ignored Hank, strapping the rifle on his back and waiting for the command.

Hank led the way, pushing enough of the deadwood away to allow them to pass through the blockade.

Fernando held back and let the two lawmen go ahead. Hank kept up a constant chatter, mostly curses. Dave, the silent type, mostly listened.

The trail ran like a ribbon into the trees, a well-worn path with a sandy bottom marked by human and animal footprints, everything from rabbits and coyotes to deer and elk.

They came across the first of the dead animals within minutes. From a distance it looked like a shadow in the trees. Getting closer, they saw what turned out to be dead coyote hanging by its hind legs from an overhead branch. Its throat had been slit wide open. A pool of dried blood had formed beneath the coyote and created a kind of blood mud.

"Jesus Christ!" Hank kept saying. "Jesus Christ!"

The adjoining trees revealed more grotesque secrets: coons, rabbits, porcupines and other smaller animals in various stages of decomposition strung among the branches like Christmas decorations. Some were so old they were merely skeletons with patches of fur clinging to the bones. The fresher ones stunk to high heaven.

Hank stopped them a short time later. He pointed to a metal trap hidden in the grass. "Stay on the trail and watch where you step. The crazy bastards have set jaw traps. This one's big enough to hold a full-size wolf or mountain lion."

At the bottom of a small rise they found another trap ensnaring the badly decomposed body of a coyote pup. Crawling with insects, this one smelled like death itself.

Up ahead, legs splayed, the spotted hide of a bobcat had been nailed to a thick ponderosa pine. With its legs wrapped around the trunk, the hide appeared to be climbing the tree.

They encountered one carcass after another as they made their way up the mountain, coming finally to a meadow shaped like a bowl. Exiting the trees they approached a short fence made of long sticks stuck in the ground.

They walked around the fence into a large clearing with a clear mountain stream running through its center. Lilies and other wildflowers grew on the banks of the stream, a mosaic of blue and yellow flowers. After the grisly sights along the trail, the meadow seemed like a paradise, a pastoral scene of tranquility.

Then they spotted the cabin. It was a small, crude cabin built with logs and rough-cut wood. It stood on the far side of the meadow. Behind it an outcropping of black granite towered above its tin roof. In front a tattered canvas awning fluttered over a wooden bench and chair. Something, or someone, sat on the chair in the shadow of the awning wearing what appeared to be Kate Isaac's nightgown. The one he'd seen in the freezer.

Fernando pointed to the front of the cabin. "Is that someone sitting outside?"

Hank squinted in the sun. "I can't tell. Let's be careful."

Dave removed the rifle from his back and unlocked the safety. He stayed back to provide cover.

Hank led the way down to the stream, where he and Fernando crossed over a makeshift bridge of wooden planks and boulders. Then the two of them went up the bank toward the cabin. They walked slowly, their hands on their holsters. The sun was directly overhead now, the sky full of black vultures circling high above the meadow. They crept closer to the cabin.

"What the—" Hank said when he came close enough to see what was sitting in the chair.

The two of them stared at a dead goat wearing Kate's torn

nightgown. The stiff carcass had been tied to the back of the chair so it stood on its haunches. A black hood was pulled down over its head.

"Jesus, Mary and Joseph! They dressed the damned goat in her nightgown!" Hank bellowed. "What's that supposed to mean?"

Fernando shrugged, looking up at the buzzards flying high overhead. Waiting to feast.

Dave joined them and walked to the cabin door, a few planks nailed together and tied to the frame with rope. No doorknob or lock. He flipped open the door with the barrel of his rifle and looked inside. "Dark...can't see a damned thing."

"Stinks!" Hank said, following Dave inside.

Fernando held back a moment, not wanting to get in their way. When he did enter, he closed his eyes for a few seconds to allow them to adjust to the darkness. The only light came from the open door and three small windows, all so dirty as to be almost opaque. He saw two cots pushed up against the rear wall, next to another entrance, this one a mere canvas tarp hanging down over an opening in the logs. The canvas was faded and shredded at the bottom from long use.

He stepped forward and bumped against a kitchen chair. On a nearby table he found tin plates, food wrappers, and several empty beer bottles. Looked like the McCullers brothers had just left. Under the south-facing window a counter or workbench took up the entire south wall. Next to it stood a large gun cabinet. Not a good sign. He'd already seen the arsenal of weapons possessed by the McCullers back at the A-frame.

Dave took the lead. He circled the cabin until he came finally to the gun cabinet. Half in shadow, he poked the cabinet with his rifle and then shifted the rifle to his back. Out of the way.

"Stuck...but doesn't seem to be locked," Dave said, jiggling the cabinet door. He braced himself and yanked the door furiously.

Suddenly everything happened at once. The door flew open and the naked corpse of Kate Isaacs popped out and fell forward.

Dave screamed, falling backward and flailing at the corpse on top of him.

The rifle exploded on the floor sending a bullet ripping into the wall of the cabin.

"Ahhhhhhhhhhhhhhhhh!"

21

Fernando rushed to help Dave, who was still flailing his arms as if trying to free himself from some giant web. Fernando pulled the corpse off Dave and turned it over on its back, revealing a naked Kate Isaacs with her eyes and mouth wide open. The body was bloated and more discolored than when he'd seen it in the freezer: a dusty black and yellow color. The stench made him cover his face with his arm and step away fast. He stumbled to the door for fresh air until he remembered too late that the dead goat was decomposing in the chair outside the cabin. No relief.

Dave followed him outside and the two of them retched in the sand.

Hank appeared in the door. He removed his Stetson and scratched his head. "When you boys are done puking, let's round up the McCullers."

"I'm not going back in there," Dave said. "She was all over me. Makes my skin crawl."

Hank looked at him. "Fernando?"

"Yeah...okay. Let's do it," Fernando said.

They walked back inside. They checked the cabin thoroughly and then ripped the canvas tarp off the rear entrance and stepped through the opening in the logs. They found themselves standing before a granite cliff that rose at least thirty feet above the cabin. Footprints along a trail at the base of the cliff led them to a crevice in the cliff. About four feet wide at the bottom, the crevice provided a natural stairway to the top of the cliff. Falling chunks of rock produced the steppingstones. Some of them were still loose and looked dangerously unstable.

"After you," Hank said. "I got arthritic knees."

Fernando laughed. "Just knees?"

CRACK!

Suddenly the side of the cliff exploded and showered them with fragments of rock. They ducked into the crevice for cover. "What the—" Hank said, wiping the dirt and sand from his face.

Fernando pointed to a flat ridge forty or fifty yards farther down the cliff. "Up there. I saw the flash."

Dave yelled from the front of the house. "You guys okay?"

"Yeah, give us some cover," Fernando yelled back. "The shooter's on the flat part of the cliff to the north."

"You got it!" Dave shouted.

Fernando turned to Hank. "Stay here with your arthritic knees. Let me take care of this." With that, he started climbing up the crevice, slipping and sliding on the loose rock, until he heard the crack of the shooter's gun and the ping of the bullet as it splintered the rock just above him. He lost his grip and fell back on his left side, trapping his arm and smashing his head against the cliff. It took him several seconds to gather his wits and to extricate his arm. He heard Hank say something about blood.

Just as he freed his arm he heard Dave fire from the cabin and the brothers cursing on top of the cliff, then silence.

"Be careful!" Hank shouted. "Ole Dave might have winged one of 'em!"

Fernando felt a wetness on the side of his face. He wiped away the blood with his shirtsleeve and sat for a moment to take stock of his situation. His left arm still worked. His head wound was just a scrape. Nothing serious.

Fernando moved back into the crevice. "Okay. Let's go!"

"I'll try to follow," Hank said.

Fernando climbed up the crevice carefully. He tried to avoid loose rocks. When he reached the top he waited for Hank, who took forever to negotiate the steep incline. Fernando extended a hand and helped pull the big man up the last few feet.

"Much obliged. I ain't as young as I used to be."

Fernando ignored the comment and headed for the flat ridge where the shots had come from. He saw no sign of the brothers, but when he reached the ridge he saw a few drops of fresh blood on the rocks. One of them had been grazed by Dave's shot. From the ledge he looked out over a wide expanse of mountains, a huge area of pine-covered hills and rocky peaks. These mountains were the highest in New Mexico, Wheeler Peak coming in at 13,000 feet. They were only a few miles south of the towering San Juan Mountains in Southern Colorado. He doubted the brothers would flee into such rugged terrain when one of them was wounded.

Then he spotted a faint trail that ran along the ridge and then descended on the far side of the meadow, heading back down the mountain. More likely the brothers were heading back to their car. They would need to seek medical attention in Taos for whichever one was wounded. Unless the wound was only a scratch.

Cursing his knees, Hank finally joined him on the ridge.

Fernando pointed to the drops of blood and then to the trail leading down the mountain.

Hank nodded. "Good! That should prevent them from hiding out in the mountains." He opened his arms wide. "Look at it. Must be a hundred square miles. There's no chance in hell we'd ever find those boys in the mountains. They're survivalists. They learned that from their pop. They could live out there for weeks if they had to."

Fernando agreed. "You're right. We'd never find them."

"Okay, so let's deal with the body first and then head back to the cruiser," Hank said. "I'll call for the Christus Saint Vincent medevac. They'll take the body directly to OMI in Albuquerque. The Medical Investigator will have to do the autopsy on this one."

So they retraced their steps and climbed back down the crevice. Hank stopped at the bottom to stretch and shake his knees, as if trying to shake out the arthritis.

Dave was waiting for them in front of the cabin.

"They got away," Hank said, looking around. "Okay, let's bring out the body and lay it at the edge of the meadow there."

"No thanks," Dave said.

"Fernando?" Hank asked.

"Lead the way," Fernando said and then followed Hank into the dark cabin.

Hank, cursing, grabbed Kate's shoulders.

Fernando took hold of her feet and lifted, which was awkward because her knees were still bent from being stuffed into the McCullers' freezer.

Together they lugged the body out of the cabin and laid it on the grass. Try as he might Fernando couldn't keep from looking at her. Heavy set, with short brown hair and pubes and small breasts for a woman of her size. Fernando might have been fooling himself, but looking at her dead body now he could swear she looked nearly identical to the photos of Willa Cather he'd seen over the years. Crazy thinking, he knew. He was losing it. His mind was coming undone. The McCullers could have that effect on you.

"You want me to wrap the body in something?" Dave asked.

"Maybe that canvas over the rear door?"

Hank shook his head. "No, I'm calling for the medevac. Let the medics worry about the body. They've got masks and PPE."

Hank didn't waste any time. He called his office and told them to send for the medevac and that he wanted it here fast, as in an emergency.

Two hours later they were still waiting, sitting on the grassy meadow away from the stench of the cabin. When they finally heard the copter approaching, Hank went out in the open and waved his Stetson. The pilot dipped his rotors to acknowledge contact and circled overhead twice before landing on the flattest part of the meadow. Two medics jumped out wearing masks and protective clothing. The pilot killed his engine and watched from the cockpit.

"Gentlemen," the oldest of the two medics greeted them as he walked up to the cabin. He looked at the dead goat wearing a woman's nightgown strapped to the chair and turned to them. "That's not something you see every day. I hope that's not your evacuee!"

They all laughed.

"Sure, we thought you might drop it off at the vet on your way to Albuquerque," Hank said.

The medic laughed. "Looks like it might be a bit late for the vet."

"Yep, same with the one over there," Hank said, pointing to Kate's body. "She's been dead a few days, so be careful."

The younger medic brought a stretcher and a body bag with him The two then went into the meadow and came back a few minutes later carrying the stretcher, with a bulging body bag on top.

Hank walked to the chopper with the medics and provided whatever information they needed.

Then the chopper lifted off, its blades churning up grass and dust from the meadow. While they watched, the helicopter turned and headed due south toward Albuquerque. Soon it was out of sight.

"Now what?" Fernando asked.

Hank shrugged. "We wait. There's already a bulletin out for the Crown Vic. Something'll turn up, it always does. Just have to be patient."

The three of them started the long hike back to the cruiser. The way out took just as long as the way in because once again they had to watch for traps along the trail. Dead animals hanging from trees and hidden traps made for a slow go. As did Hank's knees. By the time they approached the last hill it was late afternoon, with shadows darkening the thick forest.

"Awww, shit! What's that?" Hank asked, as they left the protection of the pines and saw smoke.

Thick, black smoke swirled over the rise where the cruiser and the two other cars were parked. Fernando and Dave ran quickly over the hill, leaving Hank to hobble after them on his bad knees.

Coming over the rise they saw the Crown Vic burning, not the cruiser. But the cruiser hadn't entirely escaped the McCullers wrath. All four tires were flat, punctured by some large instrument, probably the same one that had punctured Rachel's tires at the ski basin. They looked around for the third vehicle, the blue Passat that had been parked in front of the Crown Vic. But the Passat was gone.

Hank joined them. "Well I'll be go to hell," he said in disgust.

"Looks like they took off in the Passat," Dave said.

Hank laughed. "Hah! Probably to a chop shop in Questa or down in Española, if I know the McCullers."

Dave nodded.

"Don't just stand there!" Hank said. "Call the fire department and then call the office and tell them to send a goddamned tow truck."

Dave made the calls, which took time because both requests required a good deal of explaining. By then the black smoke had begun to dissipate, leaving the Crown Vic a burned out hulk of blackened steel and melted rubber.

Then the three of them sat on a patch of grass and waited, staring at the remains of the Crown Vic. They waited a full thirty minutes before they heard a siren and saw a fire truck coming down the lane. Hank got up and waved at the truck as it approached. Two firefighters jumped out and said a few words to Hank and then doused the burned out car with a water hose so it wouldn't reignite. Then the firefighters jumped back in the truck and took off again. Not another word exchanged.

The tow truck took even longer to appear. They waited another hour before the truck arrived. It took another half hour to load the cruiser and haul it out to the highway, all four of them scrunched in the cab of the truck, with Fernando hugging the window.

Hank cursed as the driver shut the door on them. "Shit! By now whichever brother was winged could have undergone open heart surgery and be on his merry way!"

When they reached the highway Fernando couldn't take it any longer. He raised his hand. "Okay, stop! I need to get out of this fucking truck!"

The driver did as Fernando had requested.

Hank and Dave ignored him, everyone in a bad mood after a long day.

Once out of the truck Fernando walked alongside the highway to the McCullers A-frame and climbed into his Cherokee. All the way back to Taos he kept thinking the same thing: he would be a happy man if he never set foot in Taos again. Ever.

22

Fernando came awake imagining himself lying in his sweet bed on Acequia Madre Street. His spirts sank when he realized where he was: the El Pueblo Lodge. Still stuck in Taos. Grumbling to himself, he fought out from under the blankets and sat on the edge of the bed trying to clear his head. He remembered now. He'd been too tired to drive back to Santa Fe last night, so he'd gone to Michael's Kitchen for a quick dinner and then collapsed in bed here. Too tired even to call Estelle or Rachel, who as far as he knew was still missing. One of those nights.

He made himself a cup of coffee and sat in the chair thinking. Then he dialed Estelle, who didn't answer. She was either off to work at the Saint Francis Immigrant Outreach Program or, just as likely, too pissed at him to answer. So he tried Rachel and had the same luck. The phone rang and rang and then went to the recording. He didn't want to leave yet another message. What happened to the woman? It was as if she'd fallen off the face of the earth.

Instead of breakfast, he had a second cup of coffee and planned his day. He would leave as soon as he got his act together and go directly home to make amends with Estelle. Then he would go to his office and figure out how much to charge Rachel. He couldn't very well charge her for all his hours; that would amount to a small fortune.

Maybe if he cut the hours in half. That would reimburse his expenses in Taos and then some. If Rachel wouldn't answer her phone, then he would drive out to Tesuque and hand her the invoice.

First, though, he had to pay his bill at the El Pueblo. He walked over to the office and found the man in the Mr. Rogers sweater behind the counter. The man smiled when he saw Fernando. "Another week?"

"No thanks. I'm here to settle up."

"You keep saying that, but then you always come back."

Fernando laughed. "Tell me about it. This time it's for real. I think."

The clerk smiled and printed out the bill.

Fernando paid with a credit card and then walked back to his room, tossed his duffel bag in the Cherokee and hit the road. He drove straight through without stopping, arriving in Santa Fe just before noon. He showered, changed clothes, ate a light lunch and then left for his office without leaving a note for Estelle. He would likely be home before she was today. For a change.

He parked in the gravel lot outside his office and walked to the door. Once inside he checked his messages on the desk phone. Three messages awaited his attention. The first was from a hysterical father who wanted to hire him to find his missing daughter. The second was from the same father, no longer hysterical. This time the father was calling to tell him to forget his earlier call, the missing daughter had returned. The third was from none other than Rachel:

"Uh...Detective Lopez, this is Rachel. Could you send me a bill for what I owe you? I'll put a check in the mail immediately as long as I think the charges are fair." Click.

Now that pissed him off big time. Who was she to decide if the charges were fair? He'd already reduced the bill by one half. Any further reductions would put him in the red.

Even more irritating was her constant refusal to be forthcoming about anything. He wanted an explanation. How and why had she disappeared in Taos? Why hadn't she returned his calls?

He'd be damned if he would put the bill in the mail. He would drive out to Tesuque first thing in the morning and confront her, before she had time to start her day. He would knock on her door and demand answers.

So he took his laptop out of the desk and started itemizing. He calculated his hours and then listed the prices of meals, hotel rooms, and whatever else he could remember. The total amount came out to be a number in five figures. Cutting just the hours in half would bring the total down to four figures. That seemed like a fair price.

He cleaned up the invoice and then realized he didn't have an office printer. Somehow he hadn't thought to buy one for his office. He added that to his mental to-do list.

Then he remembered that Ruby had a printer in her gallery next door. So he took his laptop and headed around front to Ruby's gallery.

When he stepped inside the front door he smelled freshly brewed coffee. He paused a moment to again admire the amazing job of remodeling Ruby had done. She'd taken Jimmy Mackey's messy, disorderly studio that had once been a carriage house and turned it into a modern gallery. When Jimmy was still alive the place still smelled like horses. Now it smelled like freshly brewed coffee with an underlying whiff of expensive perfume. Ruby's perfume.

Ruby spotted him from the back of the studio. "Fernando! Want some coffee? I just made some fresh."

"Sure, why not?"

Ruby looked like a million bucks again today. She wore a tight red skirt and a tight butterscotch blouse. A turquoise necklace added a Southwestern touch.

"Wow! This must be the new Ruby!"

Ruby laughed. "Nah, I just decided I'd dress up for the gallery. Try to look the part when I'm here. Sales have been kinda slow lately."

She brought the coffee over to the chairs near the front window and set the cups on a small table.

"Gracias," he said, placing his laptop on the table.

"So I hear you found Kate Adams," Ruby said. "Found her body, that is. Word has it there's a memorial service this Saturday at the Presbyterian Church."

That was news to him. "Really? You know more than I know. Rachel hasn't been exactly forthcoming."

"Not surprising. I mean, you're a man, you're straight...you see the problem."

"I just hope she pays my bill. That's why I'm here. I wanted to use your printer to make a copy."

"Sure. What are you charging her?"

He quoted her the four-figure amount. "I hope it's not too much. She's my first paying customer, so I'm new to this."

She waved her hand. "No problem. She's got the money. She lives in Tesuque, after all. One of those million-dollar houses."

"I do know."

"Yeah, she's a trust fund baby," Ruby said. "Have you ever noticed that most Anglos who move to Santa Fe have trust funds? Even the artists and the counterculture types."

He laughed. "I have noticed."

"Well, are you going to tell me what happened in Taos or do I have to pry it out of you bit by bit? How did Kate Adams end up dead?"

So while they drank their coffee, he told her about finding Kate's body and their pursuit of the McCullers Brothers. He even told her about the corpses on the McCullers property. Everything that he could remember. He knew that Ruby of all people would appreciate the macabre details.

"Jesus!" Ruby said. "Sounds ghastly. So these brothers killed Kate?"

"That's the theory. Sheriff's tracking them down now."

After coffee, Ruby helped him hook up his laptop to her printer. When he left the gallery some time later he had Kate's bill in hand. He intended to present the bill in person.

C.O.D.

23

Fernando turned into Rachel's driveway in Tesuque at eight o'clock sharp. He worried at first because he didn't see her BMW until he stepped out of the Cherokee and peeked through the garage window, where the Beamer was parked. Relieved, he walked up the sidewalk between the garage and guesthouse to the front door and rang the bell. No one answered, so he rang again. He refused to go away empty handed. Then he knocked loudly and stood back from the door considering. He was about to go around back and try the kitchen door when he heard footsteps inside. Slow, heavy footsteps. He wondered if she'd been sleeping.

When the door opened a disheveled Rachel stood looking at him. She didn't bother to hide her surprise, not to mention her disappointment. She continued to stare, saying nothing. She wore black tights and a sleeveless T-shirt. Her hair looked like she'd just stepped out of a wind tunnel.

"I brought your bill," Fernando said finally, to break the ice.

"I told you to mail it."

"What can I say? I happened to be in the area," he lied and brushed past her into the hallway.

She turned and watched him walk into the study and sit down in a leather chair.

"You owe me an explanation," he said.

She closed the door and joined him in the living room, sitting on a leather sofa across the room from him. She checked her watch. "What do you mean?"

"What happened to you in Taos? I looked for you at the El

Pueblo—you never checked in. And why didn't you return my messages?"

She sighed. "Well...the tow truck driver dropped me off at the El Pueblo...but I don't know...it didn't look very clean. A dump, really. So I walked down Kit Carson to the Sagrado, where Kate and I had stayed before. It's...you know, more upscale."

"Clean," he said sarcastically.

She nodded.

"So why didn't you answer your phone or return my messages?"

"Well...I thought it might be the kidnappers calling."

"And my messages?"

"I didn't know what to say. I didn't have any news. To tell you the truth, I don't know what I'm doing...I'm very stressed...and confused."

"Confused about what?"

"About what to do next. Without Kate."

He began to feel a twinge of sympathy for her, even if she was maddeningly evasive.

He looked around the room, suspicious of what he saw. The place was a mess, topsy-turvy compared to how it looked on his last visit. Everything out of place.

"Okay," he said. "Here's my bill."

She accepted the itemized invoice and looked it over quickly. "Fine. Let me get you a check."

While she was gone he walked over to examine a duffel bag on the coffee table. Is that how she'd planned to transport the ransom money? He was about to unzip the bag when she returned.

"Here," she said, handing him a check.

"Thanks."

She glanced at her watch again. Then she stood rigid staring at him, not sitting back down. It was clear she wanted him to leave. Just like that. Without any explanation.

Standing next to her he noticed a red ring around her neck. A red indentation in her skin. As if something tight had been digging into her flesh. Something like the drawstring on the hood used by the McCullers to kill Kate.

Now he was worried. What wasn't she telling him?

"Are you sure you're okay? The McCullers brothers are still on the loose. The sheriff hasn't found them yet."

She glanced away. "No...I'm okay."

He knew she was lying. "Just be careful. If you need me, give me a call. I'm only a few minutes away. Do you understand? I can help you if you let me."

"I know...I'll call you."

She escorted him to the door and closed it behind him.

He walked out to his Cherokee and sat for a moment. He didn't like what he'd just seen. Something was wrong. She kept checking her watch as if she were expecting someone.

He couldn't just leave. He felt a certain obligation to the woman. So he pulled out of the driveway and proceeded down the street into Tesuque. When he came to an open field he stopped and parked on the side of the street. Then he grabbed his binoculars and walked across the field to the ridge that ran along the rear of the properties.

Climbing through piñon and juniper he found a narrow trail at the top of the ridge. He followed the trail back toward Rachel's house. It took no more than five minutes to reach her backyard. From the top of the ridge he looked directly through the bank of windows and French doors on her south-facing patio. Using his binoculars, he saw Rachel pacing in her living room, walking back into the kitchen and then retracing her steps. She kept glancing at her watch as she paced, never sitting down or moving to another room.

He sat down on the side of the hill to watch. He wasn't disappointed.

Less than thirty minutes later a car pulled into her driveway, a small sedan painted an odd purple color. That would be Kate's blue Passat retooled by a chop shop.Two men jumped out of the sedan. He didn't have to look too closely to identify them. It was the McCullers brothers, as he expected. Travis led the way, disappearing down the walkway between the garage and guesthouse, with younger Johnny following along behind.

Switching to the windows he saw Rachel go to the front door and then the three of them coming back into the living area. Travis seemed to be shouting at Rachel until she handed him the duffel bag. He unzipped the bag and dumped the contents on the coffee table. Money, lots of money, all wrapped in tight bundles of bills. He appeared to count the money quickly and then shoved it away with a swipe of his hand.

Suddenly Travis exploded, motioning with his hands and raging at Rachel, who cowered meekly by the windows. She tried to say something but he backhanded her, sending her crashing into the window shade and then reeling to the floor. He picked her up by her hair and backhanded her again, this time harder. Screaming, she fell heavily on the coffee table smashing a glass vase and tray. She lay motionless among the glass shards on the floor.

Fernando had seen enough. No more. He hurried down off the ridge into the backyard. He wanted to surprise the brothers, so he went around to the front door and left his binoculars on the porch. Then he crept inside the open door hearing Travis bellowing in the living area.

"Fucking bitch is trying to double-cross us, Johnny! This is only half of what I told her to bring."

"Fuckin' bitch," Johnny repeated.

"Look around the house. Take anything that looks valuable. Wait, give me a hood."

Johnny pulled a black hood out of his rear pocket.

At that moment Fernando stepped into the room, his Smith & Wessen in hand. "Leave her alone!"

Travis pivoted to face him. "You! What the fuck? You must be some kind of slow learner."

Without a weapon, Travis didn't appear much of a threat. He was too thin, too wiry, with a sunburned craggy face and long shaggy hair.

Fernando smiled. "What do you want with the hood? Are you planning to suffocate her like you did Kate Adams? When you broke into her room at the Luhan House?"

"Hah! She wasn't in her room—she was walking around outside in her nightgown. We found her behind the house."

"And you strangled her."

"No! We didn't strangle her. Jensen killed her. He was supposed to gag and tie her up so we could ransom her, but he pulled the drawstring too tight. She was already dead when we got there."

"Tom fucked her up," Johnny added, with a smile fixed on his round face.

"Clumsy fucker!" Travis said.

Johnny chuckled.

With that, Travis reached down and lifted Rachel by her hair. Then he pulled a pistol out of his waistband and turned to face Fernando. "Now, smart guy, put your gun down or I'll blow her brains out. Now!"

Fernando hesitated for a moment and then did as he was told, placing his gun on the floor.

"Good boy," Travis said. He let go Rachel's hair and shoved her away. She crashed back on the floor.

"What are you going to do now, shoot me? I'm a former Santa Fe police detective. You kill me and they'll hunt you down like a dog. They'll kill you and your brother both. Is that what you want? For Johnny?"

"We ain't afraid of cops," Johnny said.

Fernando noticed the bandage on Johnny's hand and remembered the blood they'd found at the cabin.

Travis looked at Johnny and smiled. "Like my brother said, we ain't afraid of cops. We know how to handle them."

"You're making a big mistake," Fernando said.

Travis stepped forward and kicked Fernando's gun away. "Bring me the hood, Johnny. Let's see if Mr. Detective here is as tough as he thinks."

Out of the corner of his eye Fernando saw Rachel stirring on the floor behind Travis. She rose to her hands and knees. Finally she lunged toward the coffee table and managed to open the drawer.

Johnny was just handing Travis the hood when Rachel reached in the drawer and grabbed the small Glock Fernando had seen in her car back at the ski basin. She waved it in the air.

POP! The first shot hit Travis in the back and immobilized him. He turned around slowly to face Rachel, her face an open wound of streaming blood under a mop of wildly tousled red and blue hair.

POP! The second shot dropped Travis to his knees.

POP! The third shot landed him face down on the floor.

"I'll kill you, you fucking bastard!" she screamed, bloodied and raging and waving her gun. With her bushy hair she looked like the gorgon Medusa from Greek mythology.

Johnny screamed and put both hands over his ears. Then he turned and ran out of the house.

"You bastard, you fucking animal, I'll kill you! she screamed, emptying the chamber into Travis' now twitching body. Finally she crawled over and lunged at him, smashing her gun against his head until her hands were so slippery from blood that she could no longer hold the gun.

Fernando reached for her. "He's dead...he's already dead."

She looked at him fiercely. "No! I'll kill all of you...you goddamned fucking animals! I'll Kill all of you!"

She swung her fists wildly and then collapsed on the floor alongside Travis.

Fernando left Rachel on the floor and ran after Johnny. He ran outside and looked around. Johnny was heading for the purple Passat parked at the end of the driveway. He sprinted down the sidewalk between the garage and guesthouse, noticing another vehicle parked behind the Passat, an orange blur as he rounded the garage.

Suddenly he saw a black object coming at his face. His head exploded in pain. Then blackness.

24

Swimming in dark water Fernando struggled against the current. Voices brought him to the surface. He tried to open his eyes but when he did the pounding in his head worsened. Then someone called his name, so he tried again to open his eyes. This time he glimpsed two women with wildly colored hair hovering over him. Red and blue. Then more voices.

"Detective Lopez? Can you hear me? Are you okay?"

In his blurred vision the two women gradually morphed into one woman, Rachel. He'd been seeing double.

Unable to speak, Fernando raised his hand to confirm contact.

"Should I call nine one one? Should I send for an ambulance?"

So many questions. His head was spinning. He wanted to be left alone.

"I'm calling nine-one-one," she said, and got to her feet.

"No! Wait!" Fernando reached out to grab her but missed. "I'll be okay. Help me over to the side of the garage."

She looked dubious but gave him a hand and pulled him up to a sitting position. Then she grabbed him under the arms and dragged him toward the garage. Tiring, she let go and let him scoot backwards the last foot or so.

Sitting up against the garage wall, he took stock of his physical condition. His vision was blurred and his head hurt like hell and for some reason he was having difficulty breathing. Other than that, he felt peachy. His only question sitting there was why the hell he even bothered with this woman and her problems? Maybe it was time to disengage. Cut his losses.

"You don't look so good," Rachel said, adding insult to injury.

Self-consciously he reached up and touched the knot on the side of his forehead where Jensen had clobbered him. He felt a gigantic triangular welt jutting out of his forehead. He must look like he was growing a horn!

Rachel didn't look much better, with a swollen face and blood dripping from her nose. Both of them had taken a beating.

He saw his discarded binoculars lying on the sidewalk. Jensen had hit him with his own binoculars. The sonofabitch.

"So tell me," he said, disgusted with everything. "Why did Jensen and the McCullers come here? What are you not telling me?"

She stared at him for a moment and then spoke. "They came here yesterday and threatened to kill me...like they did Kate...unless I paid them one hundred thousand dollars. They put a hood over my head and tightened the drawstring to show me how I would die. I was afraid."

"Why didn't you tell me? I could have helped."

She shrugged. "I don't know. I was afraid of them. They said they would come by this morning to pick up the money, so I went to the bank yesterday. I put it in the duffel bag you saw on the coffee table. Except I only brought what I had in my checking account, fifty thousand dollars. I didn't want to take money out of my savings or mortgage the house. They got angry when they counted the money. You saw what happened."

"What about Tom Jensen?" Fernando asked.

"He must have found out he was being cheated."

Fernando frowned. "He wasn't part of this latest attempt at extortion?"

"I don't think so," she said. "He was angry when he came into the house. He cursed the older brother and yelled at Johnny, the younger one. He took the money in the duffel bag and left with Johnny. I didn't know you'd been injured until I came outside to make sure they were gone."

Fernando leaned back against the garage wall, pressing his head against the stucco to ease the pain. He closed his eyes and then opened them again, trying to get rid of the blurred vision. Northing seemed to help.

Rachel hesitated. "The McCullers said it was Jensen who killed Kate."

"I heard."

"Do you believe them?"

Fernando did not respond.

"Are you sure you don't want me to call nine one one? It might be better to let the EMTs look you over."

"No! They'll want to take me to the ER. I don't have time for that."

"What do you mean?" she asked.

"If you could help me into the house and give me a couple of Tylenol," he said. "And maybe a cup of coffee or strong tea. I'm getting my strength back. I just need something for my headache."

She helped him up and led him into the house. They stopped in the front room where Travis lay face down on the carpet in a pool of blood. "Oh yeah...I forgot about him," Fernando said, trying to shake the cobwebs out of his head.

Rachel stared at the bloody mess on her floor. "How do I get rid of it?"

"It?"

"I mean the body."

"You're going to call the Santa Fe Police and report a home invasion," Fernando said. "Then tell them you shot the intruder. When they get here tell them exactly what happened: Kate's kidnapping, the ransom, the extortion, and the confrontation today. I'll be here to corroborate your story, every detail. You don't have to worry. You acted in self-defense. Just tell the truth."

"Okay."

"The cops, whoever they send out, will call in forensics to investigate the shooting. Don't touch or disturb anything until after they leave. They'll take the body with them, okay?"

Rachel nodded and then showed him to the kitchen.

He sat at the kitchen table while she made him a cup of tea. He tried opening and closing his eyes to get rid of the wavy lines in his vision. It helped a bit.

She disappeared for a minute and then came back with two Tylenol. "Here, see if this helps. If you want something stronger, I can give you an Oxy."

Fernando shook his head. "No thanks."

She brought her cell phone to the table and sat down. Sighing, she dialed the SFPD and repeated to the police dispatcher exactly what Fernando had told her to say. Then they waited.

By the time they heard the police cruiser pull into the driveway outside Fernando was drinking his second cup of tea. The Tylenol had kicked in and his headache had faded to soreness.

He accompanied Rachel to the front door, recognizing his former colleague Manny walking up the sidewalk. The youngest detective on the force, Manny liked to joke around. Over the years Fernando had grown fond of Manny, even though the younger man was a real wiseass.

"Fernando!" Manny exclaimed as he stepped inside. "What are

you doing here? Jesus, what happened to your forehead? You look like one of those characters in a sci-fi movie who has a demon or something popping out of his head!"

Fernando laughed and then explained the situation. "I can corroborate everything Rachel tells you."

Manny stared at Rachel's wild red and blue hair. Rachel stared back at the young, clean-cut detective.

"Yeah?" Manny asked, looking at the body of Travis on the floor. "I'm listening."

25

By the time Fernando hit the road it was half past one. Manny and then Miguel and Teresa in forensics had detained them for over four hours, taking statements and collecting evidence. After forensics left with the body of Travis, Rachel gave him a ride to his Cherokee parked further down on Bishop's Lodge Road. "So what are you going to do?" she asked when she dropped him off.

"I'm going to find Tom and Johnny," he said. "We need to talk."

Rachel looked dubious. "Are you sure? Maybe we should let the police find them. I should have called the police earlier."

She tried to stop him, but he waved her off. Instead he climbed into the Cherokee and drove back to the highway headed north.

Now, topping the hill into Española, he realized he hadn't eaten since early this morning. So he pulled into a Wendy's drive-thru on the highway and ordered a cheeseburger with New Mexico green chile.

He parked in a corner of the lot and dialed Hank on his cell phone, attempting to eat at the same time. "Hank?" he asked when the gruff voice answered, dropping green chile and mustard in his lap. "Fernando here. I have some news."

"Yessir, I heard. I just got off the phone with Detective Rodriguez. He wanted me to verify your story, which I did."

Fernando struggled with a wad of napkins, wiping the green chile and mustard off his lap. He cursed under his breath.

"This whole thing just keeps getting worse every time I hear from you people," Hank continued. "I don't know what the hell to make of Tom Jensen now. You think he killed Kate?"

"I don't know, but I intend to find out," Fernando said. "I'm on my way up to Taos now."

"Okay, but watch yourself. We have three people dead already—we don't need a fourth."

"I'll be in touch," Fernando said, and clicked off so he could finish eating his cheeseburger, which was dripping on the floorboard now.

He wolfed down what remained of his cheeseburger and then jumped out of the Cherokee and brushed himself off. He looked like he'd just crawled out of a dumpster. His shirt and trousers were stained with mustard and cheeseburger juice and he had a horn growing out of his forehead.

He got back in the Cherokee and pulled out on the highway. On the outskirts of Española he drove by a couple of used car lots. Out of the blur of vehicles he caught a glimpse of an orange Jeep, a Wrangler. Instantly he hit the brakes. He slowed down and turned around at the next turning lane. Headed back, he saw the Wrangler parked in front of the office, a small building no bigger than a shed. He turned into the lot and coasted up to the office.

He didn't know the license number, but the Wrangler looked exactly like Tom's, with a sun-faded roof and front hood.

A plump balding man came out of the office to meet him. "Looking to trade in your Cherokee?" the man asked, noticing the damage to its front fender. He ran his hand over the damaged fender.

"No, I'm looking for the guy who owns the orange Wrangler over there," Fernando said.

The bald man smiled. "You're looking at him. Guy who owned it stopped by this morning and sold it to me. I can give you a good deal, if you're interested. Runs like it's new."

"No thanks. Did the owner trade it in for another Jeep?"

"Nah, he just sold it. He called someone to pick him up and give him a ride to Taos. Him and his passenger, a chubby little guy who didn't look right, if you know what I mean."

Fernando glanced around the lot, thinking. "What did he look like—this person who gave them a ride?"

"Sure. He was an Indian. That's all I know about him. Why?"

Fernando smiled. "Never mind. I think I know who it was."

Puzzled, the bald man watched him drive off the lot and onto the highway. He waved.

Fernando guessed the Indian was none other than Tom's work buddy, silent Jim. Did that mean Jim was a part of the conspiracy? Too many damned questions and too few answers.

He raced up the highway mad as hell. The case was personal now. He'd been jacked around by Tom and the McCullers once too often.

He drove through Taos and turned off Highway 64 onto Highway 150 to Arroyo Seco. When he came to the dirt road leading to Tom's trailer he slowed down, not knowing what to expect. He didn't see any vehicles or activity around the trailer, so he parked in front and climbed the two-step porch. The door to the trailer was locked and he didn't bother to unlock it with his pick. Through the window he could see the trailer was in the same state of disarray as when he saw it last, with drawers emptied on the floor and furniture overturned everywhere. No sign of Tom having been there recently. So where was he?

He debated whether to continue on out the Ski Valley road to the McCullers A-frame but decided against it. That would be the last place Tom would hide out. If the man had any sense.

Instead, Fernando drove back into Taos and headed for the Luhan House. From Kit Carson he turned onto Morada Lane and pulled into the parking lot. He stepped out of his Cherokee and looked around, not seeing Tom or Silent Jim anywhere on the grounds.

He walked up to the courtyard, where two older guests were sitting in Adirondack Chairs talking. They ignored him; he ignored them. Inside the office he found Francis sitting at her desk. She had her back turned and was flipping through a rolodex.

"Knock, knock," he said.

"Oh, sorry, I didn't hear you come in," she said, flustered. Her eyes opened wide when she saw him standing there looking like a homeless person. "What happened to you?"

Fernando shrugged.

"You look terrible! Your face is red and there's a lump on your forehead and your clothes are...well, soiled."

"I had an accident, it's a long story."

"Can I get you anything?" she asked.

"Yes, a couple of Tylenol would help," he said. His headache had returned big time.

She went down the steps into the dining room and kitchen area and returned with a glass of water and the Tylenol. "Here, I hope this helps. Do you want me to call a doctor? We have one on call?"

"No, I'm fine," he lied. "I'm looking for Tom Jensen."

She shook her head. "So am I. He hasn't shown up the last couple of days. I was just going through the rolodex trying to find a phone number for him, but I didn't find one. Why do you keep asking about him?"

Fernando frowned. "I'm afraid he's in trouble. Looks like he's involved in the Kate Isaacs kidnapping and murder."

Francis sat down in a chair behind the front desk. She shook her head sadly. "I just can't believe he would be involved in something like that."

"What about Jim, the other groundskeeper? Is he here?"

"No, he called in sick this morning. We're short handed today."

"Do you know where I can find Jim? Where he lives?"

"Well, he lives in the Pueblo. That's all we know. He doesn't say much, if you've ever talked to him."

Fernando nodded. "So you don't have an address?"

"No, he's worked here for years, but we really don't know much about him. He's a very private man."

"What kind of vehicle does he drive?"

"He drives an old faded Toyota pickup. One of the small ones, whatever they're called."

Fernando put his hands on the desk and leaned over, suddenly feeling faint. He needed to rest. Good luck with that.

"Listen, you need to take it easy," Francis said, coming around to the front of the desk. "Here, help yourself to the Cather Room for the night. It's the least we can do, since you've done so much for us." She handed him the key.

He steadied himself by leaning against the desk. "Okay. Thanks. I appreciate that."

"Can you walk? Do you need help to the room?" she asked.

"I'll be alright."

She held the office door open for him and watched him shuffle down the patio to the Cather Room. Then she called after him, "You sure you don't want me to call the doctor?"

Ignoring her, he opened the door and collapsed on the first bed.

26

Fernando slept for about an hour. When he awoke his headache had subsided to a dull throb. He was groggy, though, and his vision was still blurry. He squinted his way into the bathroom and splashed water on his head. He made the mistake of looking in the mirror at his swollen face. If anything, the horn on his forehead was even larger. Maybe he should have gone to the ER to rule out a traumatic brain injury, but it was too late now.

Looking at himself in the mirror he saw what Francis meant. He did indeed look terrible. First thing he had to do was clean up and get some new clothes. He washed up with soap the best he could and then stepped outside. He had only an hour or so of daylight, so he would have to act fast. He marched across the courtyard to his Cherokee and fired up the big machine. He drove straight down to the Plaza and parked at a meter in front of the Taos La Fonda Hotel.

After feeding the meter he walked over to Taos Mountain Outfitters on the corner. The clerk, a young man with a tattoo on his forehead, greeted him with: "The bathroom is for customers only."

Fernando laughed, understanding his meaning. "Yeah, I'm a paying customer. I had an accident and need a change of clothes."

The clerk continued to watch him suspiciously. Unconvinced.

Not wasting any time Fernando grabbed a Columbia shirt and Marmot trousers. He slapped the items down on the front counter. "Can I use your dressing room to change into these?"

"Sure, if you pay first."

Fernando paid with a credit card and then changed clothes in the dressing room. He rolled up his dirty clothes and took the bundle out to the Plaza where he dumped it in the nearest trash receptacle. Then he sat down on a bench and called Hank. While he waited for Hank to answer he watched a homeless man rummage through the trash receptacle examining his discarded clothing. The man dropped the soiled clothing and walked away.

"Fernando!" Hank finally answered. "Don't tell me someone else is dead!"

"Hank, I'm in town now and wondered if we could meet...maybe get a bite for dinner."

"Hell yes! We need to talk!" Hank bellowed. "I'm just finishing up at the office. I could meet you about seven at Michael's. Unless you're tired of Michael's."

Fernando laughed. "No one ever gets tired of Michael's Kitchen. That's against the law up here, isn't it?"

"Hah! See you at seven."

Fernando deposited his cell phone in the convenient zipper compartment of his new Marmot trousers and walked to the Cherokee. He had an hour to kill. That would give him time to pay a visit to Taos Pueblo. Just on the off-chance that he would run across Silent Jim or his red Toyota pickup.

He drove up Paseo del Pueblo Norte and turned off on the tree-lined road to the pueblo, a UNESCO World Heritage Site. In the distance he saw the big parking lot for tourists and tour buses. Only a scattering of vehicles remained at this late hour. Just before the parking lot the road splintered into a maze of dirt streets that crisscrossed the high mesa surrounding the pueblo. He had absolutely no idea where to look for Silent Jim. All he could think to do was drive through the pueblo looking for Jim's red Toyota pickup. He doubted there would be many small model Toyota pickups left on the road. Most trucks were bloviated these days.

He drove down one dirt street after another looking for the pickup. Most of the houses looked the same: small frame houses with propane tanks and gardens in back. The larger community gardens were back by the pueblo, a massive four- and five-story adobe structure that at this hour was silhouetted against Blue Mountain. The pedestrians he passed by stared at him as if he were an intruder, which he was. He saw no sign of Jim's red pickup. After driving up and down dozens of lanes he gave up and returned to Paseo del Pueblo Norte and turned left. He pulled into the parking lot north of Michael's Kitchen a few minutes before seven.

Since he had a few minutes before Hank arrived, he called Estelle who had no idea he was in Taos. She expressed her displeasure in no uncertain terms and then hung up on him. He would have to make amends when he returned to Santa Fe. He told himself it was better she didn't see him now with an ugly knot on his forehead. Tomorrow he would look more presentable. There had to be something that would reduce the swelling. He made a mental note to put ice on his swelling when he returned to the Luhan House.

While he waited Hank pulled up in his cruiser. He knew it was Hank because of the Stetson on the other side of the tinted windshield.

Hank sauntered over to the Cherokee and watched Fernando climb out of the driver's seat. "Whoa there!" Hank said. "I hope you got in a few good licks on whoever gave you that lump!"

"That would be Tom Jensen," Fernando said. "I hope to return the favor."

They walked into a crowded Michael's Kitchen and found an empty table in the back. A young man with a Mohawk haircut came over to their table and said, "Welcome to Michael's. Have you guys been here before?"

They both laughed.

"Son, we live here," Hank drawled. "You must be new?"

The server blushed. He had the palest skin Fernando had ever seen. Even paler than Rachel's skin. Underbelly white.

"Yes, I just started today. Let me get you menus and some water."

"No need for the menus," Hank said. "I'll have the fried chicken plate, and bring my friend here whatever he wants. On my ticket."

"I'll have the same," Fernando said.

Hank glanced at Fernando. "What? No enchiladas?"

"Tonight I'm breaking my routine," Fernando said. "Maybe it'll bring me good luck. I could use it."

The young man jotted down the orders and scurried off into the kitchen.

Hank removed his Stetson and placed it on a vacant chair. "So tell me what happened at Rachel's house. Spare me no details. I'm all ears."

Fernando recounted the attempted extortion and then the shooting, followed by the unexpected arrival of Tom Jensen. "He blindsided me when I ran after Johnny McCullers. Hit me in the face with my own binoculars. Then he took the money and left with Johnny."

Hank shook his head.

"So I followed him to Española, where he ditched his Wrangler at a used car lot," Fernando continued. "Someone picked him up at the car lot and gave him a ride to Taos. The owner said the driver was an Indian. I'm thinking it might be Jim, the other groundskeeper at the Luhan House."

"Was Johnny with him?"

"Yes, according to the owner."

"Well, that's gonna be a problem," Hank said. "We need Johnny's testimony. He's the only witness we have."

"What did forensics turn up?"

"Nada!" Hank said. "Not a damned thing. We got no witnesses or hard evidence in the Caitlin Adams death—so far it's he said/she dead. The boys at the lab are still looking at the Kate Isaacs homicide, but there's only so much they can do with a corpse that's been diddled around as much as hers by who knows how many people."

Fernando nodded.

"Tell me, do you think Tom killed both women?" Hank asked.

"Well...that's what Travis said. Whether we can believe him, I don't know. He's not exactly what you'd call a reliable source. Especially considering what we found on his property."

"That's for damn sure," Hank said. "I wouldn't trust a McCullers if you paid me."

"What about Jensen?"

"I don't know what to make of him. He's a loner, always has been. He lives in that damned trailer up there in Arroyo Seco."

"Does he have a record?" Fernando asked.

"No, just minor stuff. Traffic violations, disorderly conduct and such. I checked."

Their server brought them glasses of water and condiments.

"So what's your plan?" Hank asked finally.

"I'm hoping Jim shows up for work tomorrow morning. Like I said, I'm guessing he was the Indian who picked up Tom at the used car lot in Española. He's likely to know Tom's whereabouts."

"Maybe."

"That's it," Fernando said. "That's all I got. Unless I go to the tribal police and ask for their help finding Jim."

"Nah, I wouldn't do that," Hank said. "They don't appreciate no outsiders coming in asking about their members."

Yeah, I know, but what's the alternative? Where else do I look?"

Hank shook his head. "I don't reckon Tom will go back to his trailer...or to the McCullers place. But fifty thousand dollars won't get him far. Maybe another used car and a few weeks in the Colorado mountains. Lots of places to hide north of Durango."

"Exactly. That's where I'd go."

"Well, watch yourself. If he's killed two people already, there's no reason for him to stop there."

27

Fernando didn't get back to the Luhan House until half past nine, thanks to Hank's insistence they go to the Taos Inn for beers. Several beers. Fernando's blurry vision seemed to be worse tonight. He couldn't tell if this was a result of the beer or the knock on the forehead. He pulled into the big parking lot off Morada and slowed to a stop. Just then clouds shrouded the moon plunging the parking lot into darkness. He could barely make out the location of the big house. Easing ahead, he parked as close to the house as he dared, given his limited vision. He didn't want to run into someone or something.

On the hill above the parking lot stood the sprawling Luhan House. As he climbed the steps to the courtyard he noticed that most of the windows were dark. The lone yard-light did its best to single-handedly hold back the darkness. He jumped when he heard the sound of an owl hooting in the trees behind him. Then he stumbled on the flagstone porch and nearly lost his balance. Cursing, he took his cell phone out of his pocket and clicked on the flashlight app. The feeble light helped him read the plaques on the doors of the rooms. Like this he eased his way along the porch down to the Cather Room.

It took him several seconds to open the door. He fumbled with the key while holding his cell phone. Once the door opened he groped behind the door for the standing lamp in the corner. The lamp bathed the worn furniture in a sickly yellow glow, making the room look even more ancient. He didn't look forward to sleeping on either of the sagging twin beds. Everything in the room looked like it dated from Cather's era, the 1920s.

He double-bolted the door and placed his holster on the nightstand between beds. Not wanting to sleep near the door, he pulled the blankets down on the bed along the far wall, near the bathroom. Just looking at the tiny bed gave him cramps. To postpone the inevitable he first went into the bathroom to pee and splash water on his face, all the while avoiding looking at the mirror. Finally he walked back into the room and switched off the light and flopped down on the bed fully clothed. He'd be damned if he'd take off his clothes in this room.

He tried to fall asleep thinking of happy times, as was his habit. Fishing with Antonio in the Pecos or taking long walks with Estelle on Acequia Madre Street. Nothing seemed to work tonight. He had the unsettling feeling that someone was watching him. He couldn't shake the feeling. So after his eyes adjusted to the darkness he scanned the room to make sure. Make sure what? He didn't know what he was looking for among the shadows in the room. When he stared at one object long enough its shadow seemed to move ever so slightly. Moving toward him, as though the room itself was closing in on him.

Sitting up in bed he noticed a painting on the wall next to his bed. In the painting three shrouded figures gathered around a kiva fireplace conducting a ceremony of some sort. Two of the figures looked directly at him, their eyes glowing in the half-light of the room. Made him nervous as hell. So he climbed out of bed and turned the painting over so that it faced the wall. The feeling of being watched seemed to subside, but to make sure he moved to the single bed nearest the door. He lay on top of the blankets with his eyes wide open for the longest time before his eyelids grew heavy.

Sometime later his eyes jolted open, awakened by a light coming in under the door. It looked like fog, or maybe light coming from a flashlight on the porch mixed with dust mites. The light swirled upward until it reached the ceiling and then dispersed into myriad streams of light slithering down the walls of the room and across the floor. He lay frozen on the lumpy mattress, eyes fixed as the last of the streams slithered under the door and disappeared outside. Only then did he jump out of bed and throw open the door.

Before his eyes the fog dissipated into a million particles that dissolved into the night. Gone.

He walked out onto the porch. The moon shone brighter now, revealing the parking lot below and the outlines of the various outbuildings on the property. All dark except for a building on the far corner of the grounds, where lights flickered in one window. He thought nothing about it until he remembered which building it was: the Pink House, supposedly off-limits and closed to the public, according to Francis. This, he recalled, was where Cather and her lover Edith Lewis stayed on one of their longer visits. Where their 'troubles' began.

Out of curiosity he stepped down and walked across the courtyard. In the darkness nothing stirred, not even the wind. He had no idea what time it was, having left his cell phone in the room. Against his better judgment he walked down the steps to the parking lot and maneuvered among the shadows. He heard a coyote howling somewhere in the distance as he moved closer to the flickering light, which now seemed to beckon him.

The Pink House backed up on Morada Lane, across the street from the Kit Carson Historic Cemetery where Mabel, Carson, and other well-known Taos residents were buried. He felt a little uneasy as he approached the cemetery, lost in shadows at this hour. The few streetlights reflected feebly off the tombstones. No wonder Mabel still inhabited the Luhan House, he mused. Mabel was buried across the street, a few feet from where she had lived for the last forty-five years of her life. Her identity was embodied in that eccentric, sprawling house. Why move on?

Cautious now, he edged up to the long porch in front, a wooden extension on the adobe structure. It was called the Pink House because its windowsills and railings were painted pink. Over the years the pink had faded to a faint shade of pink that looked like blood diluted in water. He stepped over the chain and the No Admittance sign blocking the stairway. The floorboards creaked as he crept up the steps and onto the wooden porch. The flickering light he'd seen had come from one of the two side windows. He moved gingerly over the uneven boards, worried the wood would not hold his weight. When he came to the window he had to stand on his tip-toes to look inside. He saw nothing. The interior of the house was pitch black. No sign of the flickering light he'd seen from afar.

He made his way back to the front. The windows on either side of the door were shuttered tight. He tried the door but found it locked. He looked around but then decided against using his pick to break and enter. As far as he knew the flickering light might have been a reflection of the yard light. Still, he didn't give up. He left the rickety porch and walked behind the house, along Morada. Walking through the weeds he kept his eye on the cemetery across the street. The irony of his situation wasn't lost on him: Mabel lying dead across the street while he prowled around her house in the dark looking for ghosts, or whoever/whatever was responsible for the flickering light.

Another coyote howled far away on pueblo land as he waded through thistles and sage to the back window and tried to look inside. Again he saw nothing, only darkness.

Finally he gave up and made his way back to the courtyard. Everyone else seemed to be sleeping soundly. His room was the only one with its light on.

Once in his room he closed and double-bolted the door. He kicked off his shoes and turned off the light. He needed to sleep. He was exhausted beyond anything he could remember experiencing.

He flopped down on the bed and closed his eyes and tried to fall asleep again. He lay awake, still on edge. Then he jumped up and turned the lights back on.

28

Thunder and lightning crashed overhead. In his nightmare Mabel was chasing him through a dark, stormy cemetery toward an open grave already marked by a tombstone bearing his name, Fernando A. Lopez. The thunder became a pounding on his door. He jolted upright in bed, hoping to avoid the open grave when he heard the knocking again and realized he had been dreaming. Someone called his name, a voice he didn't recognize.

"Mr. Lopez?"

Fernando stumbled out of bed and fumbled with the locks on the door. When he opened the door he found one of the young maids from housekeeping.

"Sorry to wake you this early," she said. "Francis sent me. There's trouble down at the Pink House."

"What kind of trouble?"

She shrugged and walked off.

Fernando put on his shoes and splashed water on his face, catching a glimpse of himself in the mirror. Today the knot on his forehead looked more like a lump, not a horn. That was progress, he decided.

Not wasting any time, he stepped outside and walked across the courtyard. From there he saw a group of people gathered in front of the Pink House. He recognized Francis and Hank and even Silent Jim. The other two women appeared to be from housekeeping. Hank and Francis were both questioning Silent Jim, who shook his head in response to their questions.

Hank nodded as he approached.

Francis turned to him and said, "Someone broke in last night. They left the door wide open this morning."

"We think it's Tom Jensen," Hank said. "Let me show you."

Fernando stepped up on the porch and followed Hank into the dusty, dilapidated building. The house smelled as though it hadn't been occupied in decades: a combination of mold and rotting organic matter. The dirty windows admitted little light, just enough for them to make their way through the sparsely furnished rooms. Every step caused an explosion of dust in the air.

Hank started to cough. He removed his hat and fanned himself, as if swatting the dust away from his face.

Fernando sneezed.

"Here, this is what I want to show you," Hank said, pointing toward a back bedroom.

Fernando looked inside where two foam pads lay on the floor along with a scattering of empty beer bottles. On one pad a dirty blanket had been folded up and used as a pillow.

Hank kicked at the dusty floor. "You can see how the dust has been recently disturbed."

"Why do you think it was Tom and Johnny?"

"Because Jim admitted to picking up both of them in Española yesterday and dropping them off here. At the Pink House."

"What do you mean he admitted? I didn't think he talked."

Hank laughed. "Oh he talks when he wants to...just not to everybody, especially outsiders."

"What else did he say?

"That he didn't have anything to do with the McCullers or the plan to ransom Kate. He said Jensen called and asked for a ride back to Taos and that he did it as a favor to a co-worker."

"And you believe him?" Fernando asked.

"I do. I've known Jim for a long time. He's straight as an arrow—no pun intended. I believe him."

Fernando followed Hank outside and down the porch steps. "So where's Tom now?"

Everyone looked at Fernando.

Hank motioned to Francis.

"Well, that's another issue," she said. "Our passenger van is missing. The one we use for field trips and trips to the Santa Fe airport. Tom has the keys to the van. Actually, he has keys to everything, including the garage and all the other buildings here."

"I put out a bulletin a few minutes ago," Hank added.

"So we think Tom and this other guy spent the night in the Pink House and then took the van early this morning," Francis explained.

Fernando looked at Jim. "Do you have any idea where Tom and Johnny could have gone, Jim?"

Silent Jim shook his head.

"One more question. Is Johnny an accomplice or a hostage?"

"No," Jim said. "Not accomplice."

Francis spoke again. "You know…now that you mention it, I do have one possibility. Tom grew up in Questa. I remember him telling us about his parents. His father ran a store downtown, some sort of general store, I think. Maybe he went back to Questa. He must know places to hide there."

Fernando turned to Hank. "What do you think?"

Hank shrugged. "I have nothing. Questa's all we got. At least until someone spots the van and calls in."

"When do we leave?" Fernando asked.

"Well, hold your horses," Hank said, stroking his chin. "Questa's only twenty miles from here, but here's the thing. I'm supposed to deliver a summons to Buddy Davis down in Dixon this morning. The crazy bastard is armed to the teeth. Which means I'm gonna need back-up. That'll take some time. So why don't you go on up to Questa and give me a call when you get there. I'll try to join you later, as soon as I finish with Buddy."

"Okay, I'll be in touch."

Hank started to turn away and then stopped. "And thanks for helping out, Fernando. We're short-handed right now, big time."

So while Francis and Silent Jim conferred, Fernando took the opportunity to leave. He returned to his room and finished cleaning up for the day. Then he went to the dining room for the buffet breakfast they served at the Luhan House. By quarter after nine he was ready to roll. He threw all his gear in the Cherokee, since he didn't plan on coming back to the Luhan House tonight or any other night if he could help it. One night in the Cather Room was more than enough for him. Last night had been his worst night's sleep ever.

He took his time driving to Questa. Highway 522 took him through National Forest land with spectacular views, Taos Mountains to the east and the Rio Grande to the west. He drove past the Questa Lodge RV Park into the small village, not much more than a scattering of buildings around the main drag. He passed by a gas station and a couple of shops and then pulled up in front of Maria's Kitchen. The three other cars parked in front gave him the impression that Maria's Kitchen was the hottest spot in town. At least the busiest.

He climbed out of the Cherokee and walked into the diner-style café with its long counter and scattering of tables along the wall. One old man with bulging eyeglasses was reading a morning paper at the counter, while two cowboy types sat farther down on adjoining stools. Both of the cowboys were working attentively on steaming plates of huevos rancheros.

Everyone ignored him except for the woman behind the counter next to the cash register. "Howdy," she said, a middle-aged woman with red hair tied up in a bun. He assumed she was Maria.

She grabbed a menu and walked down the counter to meet him. "What can I get for you?"

"I'll just have a cup of coffee," he said, taking a seat. "Still trying to wake up this morning."

"Hah! Gets harder the older you get, dudn't it?"

She poured him a cup of coffee and set it on the counter.

"Much obliged."

"Just passing through?" she asked.

"Not exactly," Fernando said. "I'm from Santa Fe. I'm looking for an old friend of mine who's from here. Tom Jensen."

She broke into a smile. "Tom? Sure. I haven't seen him for three or four years, though. Since his mama died, I guess."

"Both his parents are gone then?"

"Oh yeah, his daddy died several years earlier. Tom sold the house after his mama died. He said he was working as a groundskeeper."

"At the Luhan House," Fernando added.

She shook her head. "No, at the D.H. Lawrence Ranch down near San Cristobal. On Lobo Mountain."

"Really? I didn't know that."

She looked at him suspiciously. "Who'd you say you were?"

"Name's Fernando Lopez."

"Well, if you do find him, tell him Maria Thomas says hello," she said, walking away.

He finished his coffee and left a couple of dollars on the counter and then walked outside. Back in the Cherokee he called Hank right away. When Hank didn't answer he left a short message:

"Hank, Fernando here, I'm in Questa. Just found out that Tom worked as a groundskeeper at the D.H. Lawrence Ranch near San Cristobal. Can you meet me there? I can't think of a better place to hide out."

As he drove off he spotted Maria watching him from the café window.

29

Fernando stopped for gas at a local convenience store on his way out of town. Driving back down Highway 522 he tried to remember what all he'd read about the Lawrence Ranch. He knew it had once belonged to Mabel Dodge Luhan and that she had given the ranch to D. H. Lawrence and his wife Frieda so they could stay there during their visits to Taos in the 1920s. He remembered Frieda had lived at the ranch after Lawrence's death and supposedly interred some of his ashes at a memorial she built on the property. And he knew the ranch now belonged to the University of New Mexico. He'd never actually been there, but he thought it was located high in the Taos mountains on a secluded property.

He bypassed the turn-off to the tiny village of San Cristobal and continued on to the forest road known as Lawrence Ranch Road. The winding gravel road climbed gradually up the mountain surrounded on both sides by tall ponderosa pines. On the way up he caught glimpses of the twelve-thousand-foot Lobo Peak. When the Cherokee's tires skidded in the loose gravel he slowed to a crawl. The road was deserted, isolated, the kind of place where bad things happened. And if and when they did, no help would be forthcoming.

With that in mind he stopped in the middle of the road and tried to call Hank, but there was no service this high up on the mountain. He was cut off, alone. He could only hope Hank got his message.

Eventually he came around a bend and saw a chain across the road up ahead. A sign attached to the chain said the ranch was closed. He stopped and climbed out of the Cherokee and looked around.

Off to the left he saw tire tracks. Vehicles had veered off the road, through a patch of weeds and around the chain. The tracks looked recent.

He jumped in the Cherokee and did likewise, except he drove

off the road behind a stand of trees and parked. Behind the trees the Cherokee wouldn't be visible from the ranch. He put on his holster and took an extra clip out of the glove compartment. Then he locked the Cherokee and walked around the chain onto the ranch. The place seemed eerily quiet, vacant.

The long entrance rose gradually toward a scattering of small buildings at the top of a hill. The first, on the left, looked like a homemade barn built with logs and rough-cut timber, all gray with age. Logs were stacked and fitted horizontally up to about waist high; then vertical timbers extended up to the tin roof. Gaps between the logs and timbers revealed its crude construction. As he approached the incongruous structure he heard an intermittent pounding sound coming from inside.

He stood in the road listening. The pounding stopped. Then it started again from somewhere in the rear. He walked around behind the barn looking for the source of the pounding. He saw a crude wooden door, painted a faded blue color, secured with a heavy duty Medico padlock. He crept closer to the door, listening. The pounding grew louder. Someone or something was hitting the timbers inside with another object, maybe a piece of wood. He looked through a crack in the timbers but could see nothing in the dark interior other than shafts of sunlight slicing through the gaps on the southern side of the structure..

He decided to take a look inside. So he took out his lock pick and worked on the padlock as quietly as possible. It took several minutes to spring the heavy lock. He tried to be quiet, but the crude wooden door creaked loudly when he began to open it. The mysterious pounding stopped immediately.

"Who's there?" he asked, pushing the door all the way open and then stepping into the shadows.

For a split second he saw a shadowy Johnny McCullers freeze with his hand raised and holding a timber on the opposite side of the barn.

Johnny spun around and looked at him fiercely. Then he charged, screaming "Nyahhh!"

Fernando took a step forward and raised his hands. He tried to speak. "Calm down, I'm here to help—"

The impact knocked the wind out of Fernando. They hit the ground hard, sprawling in the dirt. Johnny landed on top, but Fernando lunged to the side and managed to flip the little man over. They wrestled furiously with Fernando now on top and then Johnny. All the while Johnny pummeled him with his hands and fists and then bit Fernando's shoulder.

"Owww!" Fernando screamed. "Get off of me, you lunatic! What's wrong with you? Can't you see I'm trying to help you?"

"No!" Johnny shouted and tried to bite him again.

Freeing his right hand, Fernando walloped Johnny upside the head, knocking him back. Then he pounced on Johnny, sitting on top of the chubby young man while holding his hands down on the dirt floor.

"Where's Tom Jensen?"

"He left me," Johnny whined. "He locked me in the barn."

Fernando let go Johnny's hands and waited a moment to make sure he had calmed down. Then scrambled to his feet and stood back. "Okay...then come with me. We'll find him."

Johnny lowered his head and shuffled over to Fernando.

Fernando held out his hand to shake. His fatal mistake.

Johnny seized the opportunity. Mustering all his strength and screaming like a banshee again, he pushed Fernando backwards with both hands.

Fernando lost his footing and fell back into a pile of five-gallon cans, most of them empty. He wrenched his back when he landed on top of one can and screamed out in pain. Lying there, among the scattered cans, he read some of the labels: herbicides and fertilizers.

Johnny seized his opportunity and ran out of the barn.

Fernando watched helplessly as Johnny slammed the door closed. Then he heard the click of the padlock. At that he bolted up and ran to the door. "No! Come back! Johnny!"

He heard footsteps on the road outside as Johnny marched up the drive to the Lawrence cabin and the other outbuildings.

Now what? Fernando cursed himself for being reckless. He should have left Johnny here while he went after Tom.

He stretched his arms over his head, trying to straighten out his back. Something hurt like hell. He hoped it was a muscle or a nerve and not a vertebrae. He waited a few minutes, gently stretching his back, and then began to search for a way out. The heavy wooden door wouldn't open. The padlock held it tight. No way he could bust the door away from its jam. So he eased his way around the interior of the barn, examining all the gaps and crevices.

When he found a three-inch gap between timbers he thought he might have a chance to widen it enough to squeeze through. It looked like the timbers were nailed over an opening that at one time had been a window. He needed to find a wedge, something he could use to bust open the timbers. He found what he needed on the floor under several full cans of herbicide: a two by six-inch rough-cut plank about five feet long. He moved the cans and took the plank over to the gap and tried to pry the timbers apart. He used all his force pushing and then pulling on the plank until it snapped and broke in two.

Cursing, he tossed the busted piece and looked around for another option. He kicked at the empty cans, sending them crashing against the wall. Then he picked up one of the full five-gallon cans and carried it over to the gap in the timbers. He struggled to lift the can over his head, steadied himself, and then threw the can with as much force as he could muster. The can smashed through the timbers and left an opening large enough for him to step through.

He lugged another can over to the opening and used it as a step. Standing on the can, with one hand holding to the side of the opening, he climbed up on the log frame and jumped. He landed on his feet.

By this time Johnny had disappeared.

He walked cautiously toward the Lawrence cabin at the end of the drive. Unlike the barn, the exterior of this rustic log cabin had a coat of white stucco. The cabin stood under a gigantic ponderosa pine, its front door painted a bright blue color. On one side of the front door he saw a mural of a horse painted on the white stucco; on the other side he saw a New Mexico State Historical marker.

He paused for a moment to study the terrain. Off to the left he saw another tiny cabin that must have been a guesthouse. Also on the left was a sidewalk leading up a hill into the trees where the Lawrence memorial shrine looked out over the ranch. Like a chapel, the shrine had an open door with a cross standing out front. On its roof perched a statue of a phoenix rising from the ashes, the symbol that was sometimes associated with Lawrence.

Scanning the grounds, he saw no sign of Johnny or Tom. So he walked toward the Lawrence cabin and immediately spotted the open door. The door was wide open, as though someone had just exited. He looked around the yard and the pines in back but saw nothing. He took out his Smith & Wessen and edged up to the cabin door. Then he quickly stepped inside and froze. Again, he saw nothing, only a rusted wood-burning stove and furnishings so old that they had to be the original from the 1920s. He found it hard to believe that a famous English writer would want to stay at a place so remote, so primitive.

Cautiously, he went back outside and walked through the yard. He saw another dirt road he hadn't noticed before. The road headed east through a long narrow meadow. Closer in, a fenced corral ran along the road for a ways. He looked but didn't see any livestock in the corral.

Then he spotted them. Johnny and Tom. They stood together beside the white passenger van from the Luhan House. At the end of the corral, maybe fifty yards away. No more.

Tom motioned toward Fernando and then jumped into the van.

Johnny turned to face Fernando and gave him the finger and then climbed into the van with Tom.

Fernando watched for a second as the van roared off in a cloud of brown dust. The last thing he saw before the van disappeared over a rise was Johnny's arm sticking out of the passenger side window waving his middle finger.

30

Fernando slipped his Smith & Wessen into its holster and jogged back down to his hidden Cherokee. He fired up the big engine and drove out of the stand of trees. His tires spun when he hit the dirt road, leaving a cloud of dust behind. Approaching the Lawrence cabin he slowed down. Then he made a sharp right turn onto the primitive road along the corral. The road was even worse than it looked from afar. Not a road so much as two deep ruts zig-zagging to avoid half-buried rocks in the hard-packed dirt.

The Cherokee bounced violently over the rough terrain, slamming him against the door and then the steering wheel. Finally he slowed down to a crawl, ten to fifteen miles per hour. At this speed he could dodge the larger rocks and keep his wheels out of the deeper ruts—as long as he kept his eyes fixed on the road. Coming over a small rise he caught a glimpse of the white van far ahead. The van had reached the end of the long meadow and was turning to the right. Moments later it disappeared into the deep green forest.

He had no idea where the road was leading them. East toward the ski basin? Down to Arroyo Seco? Or maybe back to the highway?

Hank might know, but Hank wasn't here.

Fernando cursed, realizing he would never catch the van at this speed. So he eased up to twenty and then twenty-five miles per hour, the Cherokee bucking under him like a wild horse. His arms, legs, and chest took some punishment as he bounced around the front seat. Only his seatbelt kept him from hitting his head on the roof of the vehicle.

Soon he came to the end of the meadow. The road veered to the right and entered the tall ponderosa pines. Once in the pines the road narrowed to little more than an animal trail, so he had to hit the brake again. He drove slowly through the trees for five or ten minutes until he saw a mountain stream directly ahead. The road curved around to the right and followed the stream down a steep hill. He was just about to give up when he came out of the ponderosa into another clearing and spotted the white van.

The van had gotten stuck trying to cross the stream, which meandered through the center of the clearing. Fernando watched while Tom gunned the engine. The van rocked back and forth in the sandy bottom of the stream. But the more the van rocked, the deeper its tires sank in the wet sand.

Johnny stood on the bank covered in mud. He brushed the mud off his pants and then jumped back in the stream and tried to push the van from behind. Nothing worked. Soon the wheels of the van were all but buried in the sand.

Suddenly Johnny saw Fernando in the Cherokee at the top of the hill. He pointed to the Cherokee and hollered.

Tom flung open the driver's side door and jumped out of the van. He stared at Fernando for a moment and then reached in the van and pulled out a pistol. He waved the pistol in the air and ran over behind Johnny.

Fernando watched them closely, planning his next move. He doubted that Tom was much of a marksman. And Johnny didn't worry him.

Leaving the Cherokee at the top of the hill, Fernando took out his Smith & Wessen and walked slowly toward the stream. He made sure Tom saw that he had a weapon. He stopped about fifty yards away. Far enough that he wouldn't have to worry about Tom's marksmanship. Then he stood on the hillside and stared at Tom. He didn't speak, just stared.

Visibly nervous, Tom continued to wave the pistol

"Put the gun down, Tom!" Fernando ordered. "Where's the money you took? In the van?"

"Is that all you want, Lopez? The money?"

"That's all I want, Tom. But the sheriff'll be here in a few minutes. You'll have to settle up with him too. Seems you killed both women, Caitlin Adams and Kate Isaacs."

Tom shook his head. "Says who? He can't prove that."

"Sheriff thinks he can. He's got witnesses now. Testimony."

"Yeah, well, fuck the sheriff!" Tom said. "Both those women brought it on themselves. Caitlin was a mean drunk and an uppity bitch. She didn't want me in her house. Told me I wasn't welcome when I dropped Kate off. When I came back she said Kate decided to walk back to the Luhan House because she didn't want anything to do with me. I helped myself to a drink anyway. Fuck her! She's the one who pushed me first. Tried to kick me out of her house."

"And then you pushed her back. Hard. Or did you actually hit her?"

"I pushed her and kept pushing her because she wouldn't shut up. Wouldn't stop with her insults. She treated me like I was white trash. Maybe I am, but I'm just as good as her. Same with Kate. When I tried to talk to her about Willa Cather she said I wouldn't understand because I was a man. Plus I was uneducated. That's what she called me, uneducated."

"So you killed her too," Fernando said.

"Hah! She wasn't so high and mighty when I put the hood on her head and pulled the drawstring."

Fernando shook his head. "You fucked up, Tom. She was worth a lot more alive than she was dead. Why kill her?"

"To shut her up! I got all the money I need right there in that duffel bag," Tom said, pointing to the white van. "Fifty thousand will get me a new car and a trailer. I can live off the grid with all the other transients and RV people. You have no idea how many people camp on BLM land—outside the law and away from pricks like you and the sheriff!"

"That so," Fernando said. It wasn't a question.

"It's the only place where you can be free—free from people who think they're better than you."

Fernando ignored the invitation to debate the meaning of freedom. "Tell me, how did you come to be at Rachel's house yesterday?"

Tom pointed to Johnny. "Travis was supposed to bring me my share, but I wasn't sure I could trust him. So I decided to drop in unexpected."

Fernando had heard enough. "Okay, enough talk! Throw down your gun!" He walked slowly down the hill toward Tom.

"Stop!" Tom shouted.

Johnny, expecting the worst, put his arms around his head.

Fernando kept walking.

Tom ran over and grabbed Johnny around the neck with his left arm and pointed his gun at Johnny's head. "You come any closer and I'll put a bullet in his head."

Johnny squealed, "Don't put a bullet!"

"Leave him out of this," Fernando said.

"I'll shoot!" Tom shouted and tightened his grip around Johnny's neck.

Johnny started coughing.

Fernando stopped. He considered for a moment. Then he dropped his weapon.

"Now move away from the gun!" Tom shouted.

Fernando moved toward the trees where, if push came to shove, he could dive into the pines.

Tom dragged Johnny over to the van and opened the rear door. Then he reached in and brought out the duffel bag Fernando had seen at Rachel's house. The bag with the fifty thousand dollars.

Carrying the duffel in one hand and his gun in the other, Tom nudged Johnny up the hill to the Cherokee. Once there he gave Johnny a shove and sent him sprawling down the hill. Then he quickly jumped in the Cherokee and drove off. Headed back to the ranch.

Fernando cursed himself for leaving his keys in the Cherokee. He picked up his Smith & Wessen but by this time the Cherokee had disappeared into the trees. Too late.

Meanwhile, Johnny picked himself up and ambled over to Fernando. "He left me again."

"You're better off," Fernando said. "Come on, we're gonna have to walk back to the ranch."

He checked the western sky. The sun was barely above the trees now. Night would come quickly at nine thousand feet. He didn't want to be caught out here in the dark.

Fernando led the way. They walked single file on the rough road. Johnny fell further and further behind, but there was nothing he could do about that. He had to get to the ranch and try to find the caretaker who he knew lived somewhere nearby on the mountain.

They followed the road out of the forest to the long meadow. There he decided to save time by leaving the road and walking diagonally across the meadow to the ranch. Simple geometry. The hypotenuse of a triangle was shorter than the two other sides combined.

Fernando motioned for Johnny to follow him across the ditch to the barbed wire fence. He held the strands of wire apart so Johnny could squeeze through. Even so Johnny scraped the back of his neck on a barb and began to howl.

"Owww!" Johnny jumped up and down holding the back of his neck

Fernando walked on ahead, ignoring Johnny, who followed along behind at a safe distance, still not trusting Fernando.

They cut through the Alpine grasses and flowers. Columbine and larkspur and native grasses brushed against their thighs and slowed them down to a crawl.

They walked for fifteen or twenty minutes until Fernando suddenly spotted the Cherokee. For some reason Tom had stopped in the middle of the road just before the last rise overlooking the corral. Confused, Fernando looked around and quickly understood why: a Taos County Sheriff's cruiser was parked down by the ranch at the end of the road. Hank had arrived.

Fernando continued walking, keeping an eye on the stalled Cherokee. They were approaching the corral when Tom finally decided to make his move. The Cherokee took off slowly at first and then faster and faster until it came roaring down the road toward the end of the corral.

Fernando stopped to watch the scene unfold. He saw Hank step out from behind his cruiser waving at the oncoming Cherokee to stop. Then Hank seemed to realize that Fernando wasn't driving and stopped waving. Instead, he pulled out his weapon just as the Cherokee braked and skidded to a stop, spewing a cloud of gravel and dust over the road. Instantly the driver's side door popped open and Tom jumped out, gun in hand.

Tom fired three quick shots: POP...POP... POP.

Hank dove for cover and landed on his big belly, losing his Stetson in the process. He quickly pointed his service revolver and fired one shot and then another: POP...POP.

Tom slumped against the open door of the Cherokee. Then he fell to the ground.

Suddenly everything turned eerily quiet. Not a sound.

Finally Hank stood up unsteadily and hobbled over to where Tom lay in the dust. He squatted down to take Tom's pulse. Then he turned and hobbled back to his cruiser. He slammed the door closed and turned to the police radio.

Fernando stepped through the fence and climbed back up to the road. He walked cautiously toward the Cherokee, not knowing if Tom was dead or only wounded. Also, he didn't want to disturb any evidence forensics would want to collect.

Tom lay face down in the sand, his long gray ponytail twisted to one side. Thick red blood pooled under his chest and abdomen. Both Hank's bullets had found their mark.

Hank hobbled over and pointed to Tom. "I guess we know who killed Kate Isaacs."

"And Caitlin Adams," Fernando added.

Hank ran his big hand over a bullet hole in the open door of the Cherokee. One of his bullets had penetrated the door and then hit Tom. "Sorry 'bout that. You can have your body shop take care of it when they do your fender. Little putty oughtta fix it up good as new. Unless you wanna keep it. Kinda matches your front fender and missing mirror."

"Hell of a shot," Fernando said. "Both of them."

Hank laughed. "At first I thought it was you driving the Cherokee. I ran out on the road waving like a damned fool. Lucky me Tom couldn't hit a barn if he was standing inside."

"Yeah, well, he admitted to killing Kate right before he jacked me," Fernando said. "In fact he was proud of it. And Caitlin. Said they were a couple of uppity bitches who brought it on themselves."

"Confirms what you said earlier. Good."

Fernando pointed to Johnny still trudging down the road. "I got Johnny. Tom had him locked in the barn when I arrived."

"Yeah, ole Tom turned out to be a real prince of a fella," Hank said, looking into the Cherokee. "You might want to grab whatever you need in there before forensics arrives. I'll need to keep the duffel bag until the investigation is finished. Then I'll return it to what's her name, Rachel?"

"What about the Cherokee?"

Hank shook his head. "Not a problem. They'll just take some photos. You should be able to drive off into the sunset. If not, I'll give you a ride to the El Pueblo. They're always glad to see you."

Fernando laughed.

While they talked Johnny walked up to the Cherokee and looked down at Tom's body. "Oh no, another ghost."

Fernando started to say something and then decided against it. Instead, he turned to Hank.

"As if we didn't have enough ghosts in these parts already," Hank said.

31

Several days later Fernando still had not taken his Cherokee to a body shop. He kept postponing, wondering if a vehicle with a bullet hole in the driver's side door would be good advertising for a private investigator. If so, he could make sure to park it near his sign every morning. He couldn't decide. Ruby, on the other hand, claimed it was keeping customers away from her gallery. Business had been slow since his return from Taos, she pointed out.

He sat at his desk mulling over this existential dilemma when his cell phone rang. He could tell who was calling by the pause at the other end of the line. "Uh...detective Lopez?"

"Good to hear from you, Rachel! How are you feeling?" he asked.

She sighed. "Like a truck ran me over."

"I believe it. You took a lot of punishment."

"Yeah...so I wondered if we could meet for coffee today. I'd like to talk to you about what happened."

"Sure. Where and when?"

"How about the coffee shop on Marcy? Are you free in about fifteen minutes?"

"Yeah...I'm just reading the *Independent*. Or trying to. Anything to get me away from that!"

She laughed. Sort of. The closest thing to a laugh he'd heard from her.

He finished reading the newspaper and then tossed it in the trashcan on his way out the door. He had an appointment at 2 p.m. with a woman who suspected her husband of infidelity. That would give him a good hour with Rachel, more than enough time to rehash the events of the past week or so. He drove the Cherokee, with its dented fender and honorable bullet hole, down to the Paseo and around to Marcy Street. He found a parking spot near the office of the *Independent* and walked down to the coffee shop. He saw Rachel sitting at a table near the window. She waved at him. Almost friendly.

Once inside he went directly to the counter and ordered a regular coffee. None of the fancy stuff for him. He dumped sugar and cream into the steaming cup and went to join Rachel, who was already sipping her foamy mixture of coffee and whatever flavored crap the barista had added to her cup. Approaching the table he couldn't help but stare at her face—still swollen and discolored, although a generous layer of make-up covered most of the worst bruising.

"I know, it looks horrible," she said, noticing his stare.

"No, it looks like it's healing nicely," he lied, taking a seat. "I mean, you survived a vicious attack."

Rachel nodded, looking down at her cup. "I wanted to thank you in person for saving my life twice. I never had a chance to thank you in Taos or in Tesuque. I didn't want you to think I wasn't grateful."

"No, no, I never thought that. And anyway, I think you saved the day in Tesuque. You shot Travis and prevented him from killing all of us. Which I'm sure he would have done."

She smiled ever so slightly. "Well, I also wanted to apologize to you for my outburst the other day. I snapped. I guess the McCullers brought back all my bad feelings toward men. They were such brutes...I don't know...they reinforced my general opinion of men."

Fernando laughed. "Well...after thirty years of police work, I don't think your general opinion is too far off the mark."

She smiled. "Present company excepted, of course."

"Of course," he said, smiling. "But what you say fits a whole lot of men. Nasty and brutish and whatever else you want to add. Travis certainly fit the bill. And Tom Jensen, as it turned out."

"What about the little one, Johnny?" Rachel asked.

"Yeah, Johnny's harmless. He just followed his older brother. Hank did some research and found an aunt he can live with up in Raton. The aunt thinks Johnny has Down Syndrome. Turns out he's actually very gentle, except when he's imitating Travis."

Rachel nodded her agreement.

"I also wanted to apologize—or at least say I'm sorry for not being able to save Kate," Fernando said. "I keep thinking that I should have been able to do more. What, I don't know."

"No need," she said. "If what the MCullers said is true, she died when Tom Jensen first grabbed her at the Luhan House. You weren't even involved then."

"Still, I'm sorry for your loss," Fernando said.

"You know...Kate's gone, but I still talk to her on occasion."

"You mean in your dreams?" Fernando asked.

"No, she's there...in the room. She appears right before I fall asleep. Three times now."

Fernando stared at her. "What does she say about Taos? About what happened at the Luhan House?"

"The first time she appeared she told me Cather's ghost woke her and led her outside...into the arms of the killers. Wanted her out of the room, I suppose. That's what I've been telling her for years—leave the dead alone, because they don't want anything to do with the living."

"Then why do they come back to visit us?" he asked.

She shook her head.

Fernando continued. "Why do they stick around and not go away? Go where they belong?"

Rachel stopped to gather herself, drying her eyes. "I don't know why. Since that first visit Kate hasn't said much. She just stands there watching me. Looking subdued and forlorn. Sad, really."

Fernando listened but said nothing.

They sipped their coffee, looking out of the window at people walking by on the sidewalk in the bright sunshine. More tourists were appearing every day in Santa Fe. Soon they would clog the sidewalks and streets and overrun the Plaza.

Finally Fernando asked, "What are your plans now?"

She shook her head. "I'm selling the house in Tesuque and buying something in town. I hate that house. Everything there reminds me of Kate...especially her studio. I'm giving all of her studio equipment to the college. They can use it in their communication labs. Her clothes, her books, everything goes. I need a fresh start. I've been depressed for several years."

"Why's that?"

"Because Kate and I haven't had much of a relationship recently," Rachel responded. "For a couple of years now she's been obsessed with the women she profiles. She would work all day on her research and sometimes late into the night. Never stopping. She even started visiting the places these women inhabited and trying to recreate their lives...live the way they lived. I know it sounds crazy when I try to explain it. It was almost as though she wanted to join them. We fought all the time because I wanted a life. I didn't want to live vicariously through these ghosts, but I could tell she'd lost interest in our relationship. She'd lost interest in me. I'd become just a convenience, someone to help out at home or at school. As I told your earlier, monogamy was difficult for Kate."

Fernando nodded.

"Then Friday, the night before she left for Taos, we had a terrible fight. She'd been listening to nighttime recordings of the ghosts in the Luhan House...you know, the ones the Taos paranormal organization had collected over the years? Trying to identify the voices and to understand what there were saying. All day she'd sat in her studio listening to the recordings. Finally I couldn't take it any more. I got really angry and burst into her studio. I told her she either had to end her obsession with these ghosts or we were through, finished. I'd fucking had enough!"

"What was her reaction?" Fernando asked.

Rachel frowned. "Same old, same old. She didn't get angry, she never did. Just said her research on the lives of these dead women was her life's work and that she had to do her work because that's what she did, why couldn't I understand? Was I that needy?"

He shook his head. "Needy?"

"That's how she always dismissed me. If I wanted a life, if I wanted her attention, I was needy. Too dependent on her."

"What did she say about the ghosts?" Fernando asked. "The ones on the recordings?"

Rachel shrugged. "That she believed in them and if she studied them long enough she could make sense of what they wanted. But really, how could she?"

The question hung in the air.

"Kate didn't understand that these ghosts, whatever they are, don't belong to the material world and can't be understood by rational analysis. No matter how much research she did."

Fernando nodded.

Rachel smiled. "You're a good listener."

"Hah! I listen because I don't know what to say. As you grow older you realize how little you know. About anything."

She finished her coffee and checked her watch. "Well, I better go. I have a department meeting at school in half an hour."

She stood up and extended her hand. "Thank you again, Mister Lopez."

He shook her hand and then watched her walk outside, the spring wind catching her hair in a swirl of red and blue.

Fernando finished his coffee and then headed up Marcy Street thinking about his two o'clock appointment with the woman who suspected her husband of infidelity. Maybe divorce cases wouldn't be so bad after all.

Readers Guide

1. Why does Private Investigator Fernando Lopez at first think it will be easy to find Kate Isaacs, the Santa Fe historian who has gone missing in Taos?

2. What, exactly, was Kate Isaacs doing while staying at the Mabel Dodge Luhan House?

3. What does the groundskeeper at the Luhan House tell Lopez has happened to Kate? Is this borne out by the remainder of the book?

4. Lopez traces Kate's movement the night she went missing to a party in Taos where the host was murdered. Who attended this party and who among them are the chief suspects?

5. How does Lopez discover that Kate has been kidnapped?

6. What events cause Lopez to realize that there are several people involved in Kate's kidnapping?

7. What does Lopez discover when he visits the A-frame occupied by the McCullers Brothers?

8. What does Lopez learn from Kate's wife, Rachel Wolfe, about the ransom demanded by the kidnappers? What happens when Rachel meets the kidnappers?

9. How and where do Lopez and Taos County Sheriff Hank Mathews find Kate's body?

10. When he returns to Santa Fe, how does Lopez learn of the attempt to extort the ransom money from Rachel at her home in Tesuque? What does Lopez do to try to foil the attempt? Is he successful?

11. After the melee in Tesuque, Lopez identifies the killer who murdered both Kate Isaacs and Caitlin Adams, who hosted the party in Taos the night Kate disappeared? Who is the murderer?

12. The long chase scene at the end of Taos Gothic takes Lopez to Questa and then the D.H. Lawrence Ranch in San Cristobal, just north of Taos. What is/was the D.H. Lawrence Ranch?

13. How is the murderer finally apprehended? Who actually stops the murderer?

14. Later, when Lopez and Rachel meet for coffee, what does Rachel tell Fernando about her relationship with Kate? What was the cause of the friction between the two women?

15. Lopez and Rachel's conversation ends on talk of ghosts. What do the two of them say about ghosts? If you were present at the conversation, what would your response be to each of them? Do you believe in ghosts?

www.ingramcontent.com/pod-product-compliance
Lightning Source LLC
Chambersburg PA
CBHW010140030826
48979CB00024B/1073

* 9 7 8 1 6 3 2 9 3 6 1 7 2 *